"You're ruining my life."

Her mother looked shocked.

"That's the worst thing anyone ever said to me."

"I'm sorry." Dallas felt guilty, but she also believed what she had said. "I don't want to fight with you. That's the last thing in the world I want. But you don't need to feel so responsible for me. I'm old enough to be responsible for myself."

"You think you are, but you're still very young."

Dallas shook her head impatiently. "I don't understand you. You want to be young and with kids, but you're the most old-fashioned mother I've ever heard of. You think you're modern, but you're not. You're worse than a Victorian grandmother!"

"An intensely moving story . . ." —*Instructor*

"There is no moralizing or preaching here; the truth speaks eloquently." —*Poughkeepsie Journal*

SOMETIMES I DON'T LOVE MY MOTHER

by
Hila Colman

Vagabond Books

SCHOLASTIC BOOK SERVICES

New York Toronto London Auckland Sydney Tokyo

ISBN 0-590-32424-1

12 11 10 9 8 7 6 5 4 3 2 1   1   2 3 4 5 6/8

Printed in the U.S.A.   06

I

The kitchen was hot and bright from the western sun streaming through the wide windows. Dallas threw her library books on the table and, without thinking, quickly lowered the bamboo blinds. Then she stopped and stood still. Funny that her mother had left them up. "Mom, Mom, are you home?" Dallas's voice echoed through the house, and instinctively she knew that it was empty.

Then she noticed the melting butter on the kitchen counter, the half-eaten sandwich, and the cup of cold coffee. She must have been in the kitchen at least five minutes before she saw the note. The sun had probably blinded her eyes, but there it was, a piece of yellow paper partly hidden by the sugar bowl on the kitchen table. In her mother's round, almost childish handwriting she read:

Dearest,
    I'm at the hospital. Dad taken sick.
Come over if you want to.

Mom

Dallas read the note several times. "Come over if you want to." It took a few minutes for it to sink in. "Dad taken sick." "Dad taken sick." She grabbed her handbag and ran out the door.

The hospital was an easy walk from Dallas's house along a pretty, tree-lined suburban street. Despite the heat of the August afternoon she ran. It was a long, uphill climb to where the hospital sprawled on the summit, overlooking the village. Halfway up Dallas had to slow down to catch her breath. "Dad taken sick." The words made a nagging rhythm in her head. Why hadn't he come home? Why was he in the hospital? Sick didn't sound like an accident. In all her life her father had never been sick except for one bout with the flu several winters before. Just this past Sunday, the day before yesterday, he had beaten her in two sets of tennis, and she had thought, as she did so often, how lucky she was to have a father who was so much fun. He wasn't like some of the fathers she knew, someone who came home from work and settled down to watch the news without paying any attention to his teen-age kids, except to complain about their playing their music too loud, or taking the car, or spending too much money.

Last evening, after supper, he had taken her and her mother to a special place to look for blackberries. He had known exactly where to find them. They had picked a large basketful, and Dallas suddenly remembered that she and her mother had planned to make jam that afternoon. The basket of blackberries had been sitting on the kitchen floor, and she wondered if her mother had had time to buy the sugar.

Outside the hospital, Dallas hesitated. She didn't know whether to go up the steps to the main entrance or to go around to the side where the sign pointed to *Emergency*. She decided on the main entrance, and she went directly to the information desk.

"My father, Mr. Henry Davis, is in the hospital, but I don't know where. He may be in Emergency. I think he came in a few hours ago."

"I'll call Emergency and see if he's there." The woman behind the desk looked at her with sympathetic eyes. "Was there an accident?"

"I don't know. I don't think so. My mother's note at home said 'sick.'"

After speaking on the phone for a minute or two, the woman nodded her head. "Yes, he is in Emergency. Go down the first corridor,

3

then take a left, and keep walking. You'll see the desk there."

"Did they say what it is?" Dallas asked.

"No. You'll find out," the woman said kindly.

Dallas walked swiftly down the long corridor. She averted her head when she saw a figure, wrapped in blankets, wheeled out of an elevator on a stretcher.

She hadn't gotten as far as the desk when her mother came running up to her. "Dallas . . . Dallas. . . ." Her mother threw her arms around her and held her close. "It's awful, it's just awful. . . ."

Dallas held on to her mother and tried to quiet her sobs.

"I'm all right. I've really been all right. I'm so glad you're here," her mother sobbed. "I was just going to call the house. . . ."

"I was at the library. Tell me, what happened?" Dallas led her mother to a bench where they could both sit down.

"They called me from his office." Mrs. Davis finally spoke in a quiet voice and looked at her daughter. "He had a heart attack, darling. I almost can't believe it. He's so young. Only forty-one. . . . But that should be in his favor, shouldn't it?" She looked at Dallas pleadingly, asking for reassurance.

"I — I guess so." Dallas felt stunned. "How could he have a heart attack? Just like that, out of the blue? He's always been so healthy —"

4

"I know. And he's done all the right things.
. . . I mean he took care of himself, and I took
care of him. I thought he'd live to be a hundred. . . ."

"But Mom, he's not going to *die!* Lots of
men have heart attacks and go on living. He's
strong, and young, and healthy. Mom, he can't
die."

"People die, Dallas." Mrs. Davis spoke
softly. Her face was stricken with pain, and
she closed her eyes.

"What did the doctor say? Where is he now?
What are they doing for him? Can I see him?"
Dallas asked one question after another, not
waiting for the answers.

"He's still in the Emergency Room. I think
they're going to take him to Intensive Care.
The doctor doesn't say anything. He says
they're doing everything they can. He's in an
oxygen tent. He's unconscious, darling." Her
mother gripped her hand hard. "I'm afraid
he's in a coma."

"Mom, he's going to be all right. He has
to be. He just has to be." Dallas held her
mother's hand between her own two, and they
sat there, waiting.

They waited throughout the night. At vari-
ous times the doctor came out to speak to
them. Once Dallas persuaded her mother to
go out for sandwiches and coffee. Another time
Dallas brought up more coffee and sandwiches

to the waiting room. Once her mother was allowed to go into the Intensive Care Unit to see her husband and came out looking like death herself. In the early hours of the morning, Dallas begged to be able to see her father.

A nurse led Dallas through long corridors and then into a deadly quiet room. Her father was on a bed flat on his back, enclosed in a transparent tent, with a tube attached to his arm and a machine making a frightening, erratic ticking as it monitored his heartbeat. "Dad, Daddy. . . ." Dallas whispered softly, but the figure on the bed made no response. His eyes were closed and his breathing was hard. Dallas stood as close as she could get, looking at him. She was aching to bend down to kiss him, but she knew she could not. She felt that if she concentrated hard enough he would know that she was there.

In a few minutes the nurse tapped her on the shoulder and said her time was up. Dallas didn't want to go back to her mother. She was afraid that her father was dying, and she wanted to be alone to try to digest the thought. How could a person be alive and well one day, and the next be dying? It was too frightening to grasp. Her father's parents, her grandparents, were healthy and active. How could their son be dying? Old people died, not someone young and strong like her father. . . .

But he did. At twenty minutes past seven

in the morning the doctor came into the waiting room. Dallas knew the minute she saw his face what he had come to tell them.

He nodded his head at their questioning faces. "I'm sorry. We did everything we could for him. He wasn't in pain. He died quietly. Do you want to see him?"

Mrs. Davis nodded her head. They followed the doctor down the corridors again. He didn't look any different in death, except that there was no tent or tube or machines. Dallas had never seen a dead person before, and she was almost afraid to look at her father. But he looked exactly the same. His face was still suntanned — she remembered how he had taken off his hat on the tennis court on Sunday, saying he wanted to get more sun — and when she timidly bent down to kiss him, his forehead was warm. Her mother whispered to her, "Darling, do you mind? I'd like to be alone with him for a few minutes."

Dallas squeezed her mother's hand and left her. She felt peculiar that she wasn't crying. She ought to be crying. Instead her throat felt dry and choked up. She sat in the waiting room, wondering what was wrong with her. It was as if she were trying to figure out *what* to feel instead of experiencing the feeling itself. The only thing she felt was stunned.

After a while her mother came to her. Her mother, all of a sudden, looked very young.

She had no makeup on, and her face was pale and drained, but with her bare legs and sandals, short skirt, and hair bleached by the sun and falling to her shoulders, she looked like a kid. She looks like me, Dallas thought, even her figure's almost as good as mine. The only difference is her eyes are brown and mine are blue. . . .

"Dallas!" Then her mother burst into tears, and Dallas felt the tightness in her own throat break, and she was sobbing with her mother. They clung to each other and wept.

Viola Waters, her mother's closest friend, was pouring coffee for the three of them. It was late in the afternoon, and the kitchen counters and refrigerator were filled with casseroles and cakes, tinned hams, fruit, cookies, cheeses, and wine, all food that friends and neighbors had been bringing during the day. "There's enough food here to feed an army," Vi said, sitting down at the kitchen table with Dallas and her mother. She was a round-faced, energetic woman, mother of two sons, one, Victor, who had graduated from high school with Dallas in June, and the other Andy, who was a junior in college.

"I suppose we'll need it," Mrs. Davis murmured. She had sat back and seemed relieved to let her friend and Dallas take care of what had to be done. Even when the undertaker had arrived and the time came to select a casket, Mrs. Davis had said, "You decide, Dallas. You and Vi. Something very good but simple. I can't even think about it." Dallas had let Vi talk to the undertaker. She didn't want any part of it either and had quietly gone up to her room until he left.

Everyone had been extremely solicitous of Mrs. Davis. Dallas admired the way her mother had held up during the day, keeping herself under control, and breaking down only when her father's partner in their architectural firm had arrived. Then she had clung to him and wept unconsolably. Dallas kept herself busy pouring coffee, serving cake, answering the phone, and a few times she had thought, My mother lost her husband, but no one seems to remember that I've lost my father. She had gone into the bathroom and cried softly to herself, ashamed of her horrid thought. Maybe the loss was worse for her mother, but her father hadn't been just an ordinary father, and no one in the world, not even her mother, knew of the special relationship they had had. She wanted to scream when one neighbor, someone she had never liked anyway, said, "You'll have to take care of your mother now, Dallas. She'll be all alone." She hadn't one word of sympathy for Dallas's loss.

"Is there anyone else that should be called?" Vi asked, consulting the list of names in front of her. "Bob will meet Hank's parents at the airport," she said, Bob being her husband. "And are you sure you don't want to call your mother?" she asked Mrs. Davis.

Ellen Davis shook her head. "No, I'll call her in a few days. I don't think I can cope with my mother right now."

"You two never did get along, did you? Well, you do what's best for you, Ellen. Your mother'll probably be furious, but don't worry about that now."

"I don't intend to," Mrs. Davis said. "Dallas, is Jennifer going to spend the night here?"

"I'll be glad to stay if you want me to," Vi said before Dallas had a chance to answer.

"No, thank you. You have your family at home. Jennie is such a dear girl, and it will be nice for Dallas."

"I don't need anyone. I'd just as soon be alone, but if you'll feel better. . . ." Jennifer Kinney was Dallas's best friend, but she did want to be alone.

"I think it will be nice to have her here."

Dallas took one sip of her coffee and put it aside. She didn't want another cup of coffee. Abruptly she stood up. "Mom, do you mind if I go out for a little while? I just want a little air. You're not leaving right away, are you, Vi?"

"No, you go ahead. It will do you good. Go for a walk. I'll be here."

Mrs. Davis reached out her hand to Dallas. "Don't be too long, love. I'll worry about you."

Dallas bent down to kiss her mother. "I'll just be a short while."

Dallas was glad that there was no one around when she went outside. It had been a hot day, but now the sky had clouded over and there was a slight breeze. Dallas walked past the carefully kept lawns, the neat clapboard houses, and the gardens blooming with marigolds, petunias, roses, and phlox to the end of the street. There she turned into a narrow dirt path that led through a patch of woods. In these woods her father had shown her, years ago, how to look for mushrooms, had taught her the names of the wild flowers, and, one summer, had helped her build a tree house. She wished the tree house was still there and she could sit in it forever.

She found a clearing and sat on the trunk of a fallen, dead tree, her head cupped in her hands. Her feelings were still too deep and entwined within her to dig out and examine. What she felt was a heavy weight; she had never known that "a heavy heart" was an actual physical feeling. She couldn't imagine life at home without her father. He was the one who had brought vitality into the house. He liked to have people around. He was always suggesting that they ask someone over or go on an outing somewhere. Her mother was more withdrawn, moodier. She didn't like to give parties—she said they made her nervous —and when her parents did have them, her father was the one who did most of the work, with Dallas helping.

But I'm not going to be home this year, Dallas thought. She had been accepted at Dartmouth in New Hampshire and was supposed to leave their Connecticut home in early September. Her heart dropped. She couldn't go away now. The thought struck her like a blow. But I don't want to stay home, I don't want to stay home! When she had gone to visit Dartmouth with her parents, her father had fallen in love with the place. "It's just right for you," he said. "I hope you get in." He had been as excited as she when her acceptance letter arrived.

Dallas started to cry, softly at first and then in loud, body-wrenching sobs. "I'm selfish, thinking of myself. I'm a terrible person, but Daddy, Daddy, what am I going to do?" She felt that her father was close to her here in their woods, and she knew that this clearing was going to be her place. It was where she would come to grieve and to find some comfort in being alone with her thoughts and her feelings, where she could think of her father and herself apart from the rest of the world.

Dallas cried until she felt worn out. She

would have liked to stretch out on the moss beside the tree trunk and go to sleep, but wearily she pulled herself up. The sun had come out again from behind the clouds and was lighting up the horizon. It was low, seeming to touch the treetops in the distance, and Dallas hurried down the path. She had stayed away too long. Her mother would be upset. When Dallas got to the street, she ran the long block to her house.

2

The house was filled with people, as if a party were going on. A long table was laden with food, and some of her mother's and father's friends were drinking cocktails and highballs. Dallas didn't like the sight.

The church ceremony had been right. Their minister knew her father, and he had spoken of him in simple words of affection; he had not delivered an impersonal eulogy the way the minister had at Jennifer's grandfather's funeral, the only other one Dallas had ever attended. Going to the cemetery had been awful. Dallas hated the funeral limousine. "I don't see why we can't go in our own car," she had said. "We just can't," her mother told her. And standing by the graveside had been the worst. The sun was too bright, the day too beautiful. How could they be lowering her father in a box into the ground?

14

Many people were there, standing around silently, her mother wept hysterically, and Dallas felt alienated from everyone, as if no one knew what was going on, no one knew that they were burying *her* lively, energetic, beautiful father under the earth. Dallas kept thinking, Are they sure he's dead? What if he came out of the coma? What if he woke up and couldn't get out? For a few wild moments she wanted to scream and tell them to stop. Instead, she bit her lips and held a handkerchief up to her face, because she didn't want to watch what they were doing.

Now people were acting as if there hadn't been a funeral at all. The gathering was like one of the big cocktail parties her father liked to give, except that he wasn't there. He wasn't there to mix the drinks, to move among the guests, to ask Dallas to pass around trays of food, to give her his wide grin and say, "Just two glasses of wine for you, sweetie. And I saved a plate of shrimp for you in the kitchen. Get it before someone steals it."

Dallas watched Victor Waters, Vi's son, pass a plate of small sandwiches around, handling the larger platter as if he were a professional waiter. Dad would get a kick out of him, Dallas thought. He always said Victor was much better mannered than his older brother Andy. But Dad was dead. He would never see Victor again. Dallas turned away, her eyes flooded with tears.

Her mother looked in a daze, as if she didn't quite know what was going on. She was sitting on the sofa, pretending to listen to what someone next to her was saying, her face white and strained against her black dress. But her eyes kept following Dallas as if she were afraid to lose sight of her for a moment. At one point she asked Dallas to come and sit beside her and gripped her hand tightly. "What are we going to do? What are we going to do without him?" she kept saying. Dallas had no answer for her.

At last the people were leaving. They kissed Dallas and her mother good-bye, there were more tears, and finally the house was quiet, the way Dallas felt it should be. Only her father's parents were left, and they were staying on for a few days. Vi and Jennifer stayed behind too, and they were already busy clearing the rooms of glasses and dishes.

"I'm going to make a fresh pot of coffee," Grandmother Davis said. "You haven't eaten anything all day, Ellen," she said to her daughter-in-law.

"I'm not hungry." But her grandparents and her mother and Vi sat around the kitchen table drinking coffee. Dallas could hear her grandfather ask her mother about money — had her father carried life insurance, were they going to have enough to live on. . . . Dallas didn't want to listen. That kind of talk made her father's death seem too real. She and her mother might have to go on living without him, but she wasn't ready to accept the fact.

"Do you want to go for a walk?" Jennifer asked.

"Yes," Dallas agreed quickly.

"Don't be gone too long," her mother said, and there was a pleading note in her voice that frightened Dallas, but she pushed the unpleasant thought out of her head.

The two girls walked in silence for a few blocks. They had been friends since elementary school, and Dallas, an only child, felt that Jen was as close to her as a sister. In fact, she was closer, because a sister wouldn't have been only a week older than she. They had celebrated their seventeenth birthday together earlier that summer. There was nothing that they didn't tell each other. They could, and often did, talk for hours about themselves, their friends, their parents, about Jen's younger sister and two brothers; they had examined their bodies together when they were first developing, they had gotten sick together when they had eaten two pounds of cherries between them, they had gone out on their first dates together, they had taken a week's bicycling trip together when they were sixteen.

Dallas felt closer to Jen than perhaps anyone else in the world. She thought Jen was beautiful, the better looking of the two of them, but she wasn't jealous. Dallas didn't believe Jen when she told her she was the prettier one. Jen's black hair was thick and curly and she wore it long, her eyes were very dark, and her skin seemed to be tan all year around. She was taller than Dallas and had a full figure. "You're Mother Earth," Dallas teased her, and in a way she was, with her sturdy body and large, capable hands that could make things grow, cook and sew, take out a splinter, or handle a hurt kitten.

In contrast, Dallas was smaller, slimmer, more delicate in her looks, her hair light and soft and silky, her feet and hands long and narrow, her skin, even with her tan, more honey-colored than brown. But in her own way she was as strong and capable as Jen. She could outrun her, climb a tree faster, and beat her at tennis consistently. They gave to each other without counting, their friendship cemented by honesty and an ability for each to be herself and to laugh away disagreements whenever they arose.

"Have you thought at all about going away?" Jen asked, when they turned at the end of their street into another road.

"You mean going to college? I've been thinking about it as much as I can think about *anything* now. I just can't believe it happened. It was all so fast. I can't get it through my head that he's dead."

"I know. It's awful. It seems so unfair. Your family always seemed so close. I mean your father was different. You — I — could talk to him, not like he was a parent. I don't see how your mother can bear it. She seemed so dependent on him. You know, we've talked about it, the way she always let him decide everything, as if she wanted to stay a kid."

"I know. Jen, I'm scared. My father would want me to go to Dartmouth, I'm certain he would. He was so happy when I was accepted, right? But how can I leave her? She looks at me now as if I'm all she has in the world, and I guess I am. I can't go, but — I wouldn't say this to another soul — I'm scared stiff of staying home. I don't think I can bear living alone in that house with my mother. Not that I don't love her, I do, but I have an awful feeling I'll be with her for the rest of my life. I'll be like that Miss Jackson. She must be around sixty now, and what's her life been? Just living in that house taking care of her mother, who will live to be a hundred and fifty. She must be nearly ninety now, and she still calls Miss Jackson her dear little girl."

Jen's dark eyes looked directly into Dallas's blue ones. "You've got to go. You just have to. You can't replace your father for your mother. You have to live your own life, and so does she. Your mother has a lot of friends here in Millstone, and maybe she's not as helpless as she seems. I mean, when she could depend on your father, she did, but I think she's stronger than you think she is. You've got to go."

"I knew that's what you'd say, and I guess I wanted to hear you say it. But I don't think I can leave. I feel awful even worrying about myself now. Oh, God, why did this have to happen? I can't bear it, I can't. . . ." Dallas broke into sobs and cried with her friend's arms around her.

When they returned to Dallas's house, Mrs. Davis was lying down in her bedroom. "I don't know if she's sleeping, but go in and see," her grandmother told her. "She'll want to know that you're back. She kept wondering where you were for so long."

"I didn't think we were gone long. We didn't go far."

"I know. But she's upset now. Come back here afterward." Her grandmother patted the sofa seat beside her. "Dad and I want to talk to you."

Dallas tiptoed into her mother's room, but her mother opened her eyes immediately. "Is that you? I was worried. Stay close, darling. I need you so much now."

"I know." Dallas bent down and kissed her mother's forehead. "I'm not going anywhere. Don't worry. Try and go to sleep. You need it."

"I'll try." She spoke like an obedient little child.

Back in the living room Dallas sat down beside her grandmother. Her grandfather sat opposite, in the big rocking chair, her father's favorite chair. He was the only one she didn't mind having sit in that chair.

"We've been talking about you, Dad and I," her grandmother said. "It's early to make plans, but we have to leave tomorrow, so this is the only time. Have you thought about what you're going to do?"

"Not really. You mean about college? I don't know. Daddy really wanted me to go to Dartmouth, but I don't even know if there's money for that."

"Thank God, I don't think you'll have to worry too much about money right now. Your father carried a lot of life insurance. You're not going to be rich, but you and your mother should manage all right," her grandfather said. "The mortgage on the house is covered by insurance, and after a while your mother should find a job. There is money put aside for your education, and your mother will get a social security allowance for a dependent child. That's not the immediate problem."

Dallas looked from one to the other. "I know. I know what you want to tell me. I shouldn't go away."

"We thought that if you waited a year. You're still very young. You could stay home this year and go away next fall. By that time your mother will be much better than she is now. It's been a terrible shock for her . . . for you too, but you're young and still have your own life ahead of you." Her grandmother was looking at her sympathetically, dabbing her eyes now wet with tears. "It's awful for all of us. I never thought we'd outlive our son. . . ."

"You're right. I know you're right." Dallas could not tell them of the misgivings and fears she had. "I'll stay home. I had pretty much decided that myself."

"You're a lovely girl," her grandmother said. "You're especially precious to all of us now."

"Don't burden the girl," her grandfather said, with some of her father's wry humor and his same crinkly smile. "She doesn't need three doting parents hovering over her. Let the kid breathe."

Dallas gave her grandfather a grateful hug.

3

Dallas turned on her record player as loud as she could. She couldn't stand the quiet of the house. But after a few minutes she turned it off. Music didn't suit her mood. She didn't know what would. Dallas felt as though she were living in a morgue. The word *morgue* made her think of death and brought everything flooding back again. No matter how hard she tried to think of other things, she kept coming back to death, because the house was so quiet, so very still.

Vi Waters had warned her. "A few weeks from now," she said, during the busy first week after Dallas's father had died, when people kept filling the house with food and visits, "a few weeks from now it's going to be worse. When things quiet down will be the hardest part."

But Vi hadn't told her when the depression

would let up, when the heaviness and the quiet were going to slacken. Dallas didn't think it ever would. For the first time in her life, she realized, she had nothing to do. Summer vacations had been different. Sometimes she had worked, and there were always some friends free to swim or play tennis. But now everyone was busy doing something. Jennifer was going to secretarial school, the boys and girls who hadn't gone away to college were working or looking for jobs, and Vic Waters and some of the others were going to a nearby community college. Staying home was all right for a while, sleeping late and being lazy, but the thought of the long winter ahead frightened Dallas. There had been times when she longed to have time to herself, but now she felt as if her life had been put into a deep freeze.

Her mother sat silently in the house not wanting to do anything or to see anyone. Dallas wondered if her being there was really any help, and yet she felt that discussing her own problem with her mother would be an intrusion.

Dallas went into the kitchen where her mother was having a cup of coffee. It was ten o'clock in the morning, and her mother had been sitting there since breakfast. She'd probably drunk five or six cups of coffee by now. No wonder she didn't sleep at night, drinking all that coffee all day long.

"Why don't you call up someone?" Dallas suggested. "Call up Vi. I'm sure she'd love to have you come over there for dinner tonight."

"I don't feel like it," Mrs. Davis said. "I couldn't bear it. To see her and Bob together, with their kids. They're such a mushy family. No matter who's around, Bob kisses Vi as if they were still on their honeymoon. I just can't bear to see our old friends, to see everyone in couples. The whole world goes two by two."

"But Mom, you need your friends now, more than ever. They can help you. That's what friends are for."

"I know. That's what everyone says. I guess I'm peculiar. I'd rather be alone. But you don't have to be. I feel awful having you stay home with me this way. You should have gone away. It's not fair to you. . . ."

"I'm okay, Mom. I stayed home because I wanted to. But maybe I will go out tonight, if you don't mind. I'll call up Jen and see what's going on."

"Dallas. . . ." Her mother spoke hesitatingly. "Dallas, why don't you ask some of your friends over here? I'd like that. Your friends would be cheerful."

Dallas was going to say, but I wanted to get out of the house, and then she realized that her mother didn't want to stay alone. Her mother needed her physical presence. That was what made Dallas feel a prisoner in her own house. If she were doing something useful, she would feel different, but her mother seemed anxious to know that she was there all the time. She didn't dare suggest that she look for a job or even take some courses. Each time she looked at her mother's strained, taut face, she knew that she couldn't say a word. After all, if her mother wanted her close by, that was where she'd have to be.

"You're sure you wouldn't mind? I mean they'll play records and make a lot of noise, and you may want to rest."

"I do nothing but rest. No, I'd like it. You call them up, and then we can go out and buy some food and soda and beer, I suppose. The boys drink beer, don't they?"

"I wasn't thinking of a party, Mom. I was just going to ask a couple of kids over."

"It doesn't have to be a party. But you'll need some snacks and something to drink. We could get some frozen pizzas too." Her mother's face was more animated than Dallas had seen it in the month since her father had died.

"I'll see who's around," Dallas said, glad to see her mother take some interest in something.

Jennifer and Vic came, and Ted Bateman and Nancy Edwards and Sue Prince with her boyfriend, Joel. Dallas and Jen wore long denim skirts, and all the others were in jeans. Mrs. Davis had dressed up for the occasion in a long, purple caftan and eye shadow to match.

Dallas hadn't expected her mother to spend the whole evening with them, but she did. Apparently she was enjoying herself, and Dallas was glad. Everyone had been very considerate of her, and she had talked and even laughed, but now Dallas found herself looking at the big clock over the mantel, thinking it was time that her mother went up to bed. Dallas had brought her record player down from her room, everyone had consumed quantities of potato chips, pretzels, soda, and beer, but somehow the party, if that's what it was, hadn't got off the ground. Her friends acted differently with her mother there. The atmosphere was different, although Dallas couldn't put her finger on why.

Now her mother was sitting on the floor talking animatedly to Victor, whom she always had liked — after all he was her best friend's son — and tonight Dallas was especially glad. In the past month something had sprung up between Dallas and Vic that had not been there before. He had always been one of her crowd, but since her father died he'd been around the house a great deal more than usual.

Without any words between them, Vic had suddenly become more than just a good friend.

Somehow when Dallas needed anything done, Vic was around to do it. He had rewired a lamp for her and helped her clean out the garage. Then one gloomy, chilly day she was raking leaves, furious that they kept blowing back across the lawn, when Victor came by. She was close to tears, thinking how her father had always done this job. Then Victor made some remark about her father too, and she burst out crying. Victor simply held her in his arms until she cried herself out. He didn't say anything, but when she lifted her head from against his wooly sweater, she caught an expression on his face that startled her and made her suddenly aware of new feelings. He was no longer just attractive Victor, a dark-eyed boy who was a friend; he was someone who set her heart racing, someone who looked at her with an emotion that held both tenderness and wonder. She quickly disentangled herself from his arms and chattered inconsequentially. Victor stayed to help her with the leaves, and more than once their eyes met with that same quick recognition that their feelings for each other were turning into more than friendship.

"Do you really want me to get it?" Mrs. Davis was saying to Victor.

"Yes, come on. I'll help you find it." He pulled Mrs. Davis to her feet.

"I hope I can. It's way up in the attic someplace. I haven't played it in years."

"Then tonight's the time to start. It just so happens I have some extra guitar strings in case yours are no good."

"You are the handiest young man to have around I ever did know," Mrs. Davis said laughingly.

"You bet."

"Where are you going, Mom?" Dallas called out.

"Victor has persuaded me to get out my guitar. I've probably forgotten how to use it, but someone else can play it if I can't."

"No one forgets how to play a guitar," Ted Bateman said. "You'll remember. It's like riding a bike. You never forget."

"Do you want me to go up and get it?" Dallas asked.

"No, Victor will help me find it."

Dallas thought that her mother and Victor were gone for a long time. She turned on the oven and put in the frozen pizzas. They were sizzling hot, and still her mother hadn't come back down. What am I worrying about? Dallas thought. It's my mother and an eighteen-year-old kid! I only hope she's not showing him all those old baby pictures of me that are up in the attic someplace. In fact, Dallas half hoped that her mother *was* showing him the pictures. When they came down Victor was carrying her mother's guitar, and her mother looked flushed and bright-eyed. "What took you so long? The pizzas are going to get dried up."

"I found an old box of letters up there that I'd forgotten all about. They're from boyfriends of mine when I was around your age, Dallas. I was reading some of them to Victor."

"Pretty hot stuff," Victor said. "Your mother was quite a dame. I don't mean was," he added hastily, "still is."

"Thanks for those kind words," Mrs. Davis said, giving Victor an affectionate pat. Her face clouded over. "I guess one of the things I miss is some male attention. Hank was great about paying compliments. Even if I looked terrible, he made me *feel* attractive."

"Giving you compliments is easy," Victor said.

"Just give me what you have left over from Dallas," Mrs. Davis said, her smile returning.

She sat down and started strumming on the guitar.

"You see, you do remember," Ted said.

"Play something," the others urged.

"I'm no Joan Baez, but I'll try." Mrs. Davis strummed on the guitar for a few minutes, and then in a soft, sweet voice she played and sang an old English folk song.

"That's neat. That's really neat." Dallas and her friends applauded enthusiastically. "Give us some more," they demanded.

Mrs. Davis kept on playing while Dallas and Jen were in the kitchen. "Your mother's pretty good," Jen said to Dallas.

"Yes, she is." Dallas kept her eyes on the pizza she was slicing.

"You having a rough time?" Jen asked.

Dallas looked up for a second and then spoke while she went on cutting. "It hasn't been easy," she mumbled. "Damn." She put the knife down and sucked her finger where she had nicked it. Dallas took a Band-Aid from the kitchen shelf and wound a small strip around her finger. When she looked at Jen, her eyes were brimming with tears. "It's awful. I feel terribly sorry for her, but I feel like a prisoner too. I can't step out of the house without her. And now tonight, spending the *whole* night with us — Jen, do you ever not love your mother?"

Jen's face was serious. "I don't know. I've never thought about it. Sometimes I get mad at her, but I don't think I really stop loving her. . . ."

"Well, that's what worries me. Sometimes I don't love my mother, I think. Wouldn't it be awful to live with her and get to hate her? I never felt that way before, but then I always was closer to my father. Now my mother and I are stuck with each other." Dallas shook her head impatiently. "Forget what I've been saying. I'm just in a bad mood. Forget it."

"Do you have a thing for Victor?" Jen asked.

Dallas gave her a sharp look. "What made you ask?"

"I don't know. You've been talking about him a lot this past month. Are you upset because — well, because he doesn't feel the same way?"

"No," Dallas blurted out. Then she laughed. "I wasn't going to talk about it, not even to you, because there's nothing really to talk about."

"You two would be great together," Jen said shrewdly.

"Come on, let's bring the pizzas in before they get cold." Dallas picked up one tray and left the other for Jen.

Everyone had left except Jen and Victor. "I'll help you clean up," Jen said.

"I was going to do that," Victor said with a grin. "My mother's been telling me about men washing dishes."

"You picked the right time. There are only a few," Jen told him. Then she whispered to Dallas, "I can take the hint. He wants to be alone with you."

"Fat chance of that around here," Dallas whispered back, eyeing her mother handing glasses to Victor to carry into the kitchen.

"She'll go to bed," Jen answered, and then said good-bye and left.

Dallas thought her mother never would go

upstairs. She seemed to find a million excuses to stay downstairs, but Victor cheerfully stayed on too. When Mrs. Davis started yawning, Victor said, "You go on. We'll finish up."

"There's not much to finish," Mrs. Davis said, putting the last glass away on the shelf. "But I guess I *am* tired. I hope I can sleep. It was a nice evening, Dallas. Thank you. We'll have to do this more often. I hope having your mother around isn't a drag, but being with you kids is marvelous for me. You can't imagine what it does. . . ."

"It's our pleasure," Victor said gallantly. "Your guitar and singing made the evening, honest. It isn't as if you were an old lady."

Mrs. Davis kissed Dallas good-night and pulled Victor, who was a full head taller than she, down to give him a kiss too. "Don't stay up too late, kids. Tomorrow's another day."

When they were alone, Victor suggested that they go outside. It was a warm, starlit night, and they went out back to sit in the Davis's wide hammock.

Dallas lay on her back, looking up at the sky. Victor sat beside her, swinging the hammock gently with his foot.

"How are you doing?" he asked her after a while.

"I guess I'm okay. I go up and down. It's not easy."

"Your mother's pretty terrific. She seems to be doing very okay."

"She was tonight. This was a good evening for her."

"Anyway, I'm glad that you're home this year. I mean I'm not glad for the reason that you are," he added hastily, "but just that you are. I'd been thinking about you a lot this summer, but you were going away to college and there didn't seem to be any point to, well, getting involved. I mean I was involved, but I didn't want to do anything about it. Now it's different."

Dallas sat up alongside of him so that the length of their legs stretched out, side by side. "I've been thinking about you too," she said softly. "This last month, since my father died, I've been feeling raw and exposed, but when you were around I was okay. It's funny, isn't it, the way we've known each other for so long, and then all of a sudden something happens?"

"It's not funny, it's good. It's terrific," Victor said.

"I know. But I keep thinking it has something to do with Dad's dying. Losing him has made me take notice, feel things more deeply. He liked you. He'd be glad if he knew; maybe he does someplace. I wish I understood — "

"You don't have to understand," he said, putting his arm around her. "So long as you feel what I feel, that's all that counts. Turn around." Dallas turned her face to him, and he kissed her on her lips, gently at first and then hard, holding her close to him. They sat in the hammock swinging and talking quietly.

"I never expected to fall in love this way," Dallas said after a while. "I thought it would be more thunder and lightning, but I feel so — I don't know — so right with you. I feel as if I've known all along that this would happen sooner or later."

"I'm glad it happened sooner rather than later," Victor said.

"Hold me close." She clung to him feeling the pain of her loss diminished by the swell of her love for him.

They were still talking when they were startled by a shadowy figure in the kitchen doorway and a voice calling, "Dallas, are you out there?"

Dallas sat up abruptly. "Yes, Mom. Are you okay? Anything the matter?"

"No, not really." She came forward, her bathrobe wrapped around her. "I couldn't sleep, as usual, and you weren't in the house, so I panicked. Oh, it's beautiful out here, isn't it?"

Dallas and Victor stood up. "Yes, it is," Dallas said.

"I guess I'd better be going home," Victor said.

"Don't let me chase you away."

It was a bright night, and Dallas was sure she saw tears in her mother's eyes. "Do you want to sit out here for a while? Maybe you'll get sleepy," Dallas said. She started to follow Victor along the walk to the front of the house and the street.

"I don't think I want to stay here alone," Mrs. Davis said.

"I'll be right back," Dallas called out. She kissed Victor good-night hurriedly.

"I guess she's not as okay as I thought. It must be pretty rough for her," Victor said sympathetically.

"It is."

Dallas went back to the hammock and sat down beside her mother. "Maybe the hammock will make you sleepy." She swung the hammock back and forth, feeling very sleepy herself and aching to be alone in her bed. She wanted to think about Victor, to think about the evening, to go over their conversation in her mind. . . .

"I don't know what I'd do without you," her mother said, gripping her hand. "I'm afraid I'm being a terrible burden, but I can't stand being alone — not yet. . . . I get this awful panicky feeling. Maybe I'm still in a state of shock, I don't know. Dallas, I'm so sorry. . . ." Her mother started to cry softly. "It was such a nice evening. . . . I enjoy seeing you kids together, but then I feel my own loneliness so much I can't bear it."

"You ought to see more of your own friends. You should invite them over. Honestly Mom, it would do you good."

"Maybe, maybe. . . ."

When Dallas finally did get upstairs to her own bed, after seeing her mother into hers, she wanted to think about Victor and herself, but one sentence she had said to Jen kept coming into her mind: "Sometimes I don't love my mother, I think." The words kept persisting, and she couldn't shake them off. She fell asleep thinking how frail and ghostlike her mother had looked standing in the back doorway, and yet how strong and firm her grip had been on Dallas's hand.

4

Ellen Davis leaned over, bending her flat stomach almost in half, to apply soft-pink nail polish to her toenails. Doing so made her think of Hank, who in the early days of their marriage had said, "Never stop taking care of yourself, honey. I like that." She recalled how he had loved her femininity, how he liked to see her wear soft, silky robes in the house, and how he liked to buy her gifts of jewelry and lacey nightgowns.

What in God's name am I doing this for now? she thought to herself. Yet she felt that if she didn't she would be betraying Hank.

"Mom!" Dallas was calling her. "Victor's here for his lesson."

"I'll be down in a couple of minutes. As soon as my nail polish dries." And I brush my hair and put on some makeup, she added to herself. She liked to look pretty for the lessons.

The guitar lessons had been Victor's idea and he was her first pupil, although two more of Dallas's friends were due to start later in the week. Victor had suggested that she give the guitar lessons, and Ellen had grabbed hold of the idea enthusiastically. He didn't have to convince her that working with young people would be fun, that it would give her something to do, and that the few extra dollars wouldn't hurt.

Victor was waiting for her in Hank's study. This was his third lesson, and he was a good pupil.

"Did you do your practicing?" she asked him.

"You bet. You'll see." He strummed on the guitar and played a simple tune, hesitating only a few times and hitting one or two wrong notes.

"Pretty good," Ellen commented, "but you're not watching what you're doing."

"I want to get that dreamy, faraway look in my eyes you guitar players get," Victor said. "Like you."

"You'll have to do a lot more practicing for that."

The lesson lasted for around forty minutes, and Ellen was sorry when it was over. A few forty minutes out of a whole week to forget herself, to forget everything, and feel almost that life could be enjoyable again. "You can't imagine what this does for me," she said to Victor. "It was such a good idea of yours."

"I did it for myself. You're doing me a big favor giving me these lessons." He was looking at her admiringly. "You're a terrific woman, Ellen. You don't seem like, well, like someone's mother. I feel I can talk to you."

"I'm glad. I certainly do hope you talk to me anytime you want."

Victor looked at her with his dark, long-lashed eyes. He had his mother's Italian looks, was tall and sturdily built, his black hair worn just long enough to give him a soft look without detracting from his masculinity. "I think I'm in love," he said abruptly. "I'm not going to tell you who she is and please don't ask me. But I keep thinking about her all the time when I should be doing something else. I make up all kinds of excuses to see her. . . ."

"Does she know how you feel?"

Victor nodded. And then he surprised Ellen with a blush. "I shouldn't be talking about her to you. It's all crazy. I gotta go, or I'll be late for class. Can I leave my guitar here and pick it up later?"

"Sure, of course."

Victor left, and Ellen watched him run down the street and jump into his car. He was taking courses at the community college and also working part-time at a local garage.

"Where did Victor go in such a hurry?" Dallas asked.

"He was late for class. He'll stop by later to pick up his guitar."

"You must have given him an extra-long lesson." Dallas sounded cross.

"We got to talking."

"Oh. I don't know why he's taking guitar lessons all of a sudden. He never even used to like folk music. He was hipped on jazz."

"I guess he changed his mind," Ellen said. She studied her daughter's scowling face. "Don't you like Victor?"

"What makes you say that? He's one of my oldest friends."

"That's what I thought. But you've been acting queerly whenever he comes over for his lessons, as if you didn't want him to."

"Forget it. I don't want to discuss Victor with you."

"You brought him up, I didn't." But Dallas was gone before she finished her sentence, gone out of the house. Ellen poured herself a cup of coffee and sat down at the kitchen table. She felt as if she'd been slapped. Her first thought was, Dallas wouldn't talk to me like that if Hank were here, and then her eyes filled with tears. How awful for them to be quarreling, although it wasn't a real quarrel. Yet she had felt such a wave of hostility from Dallas. I can't bear it, she kept thinking, I

41

can't bear to go on living without Hank. It's all too much. I can't handle Dallas alone. Perhaps she shouldn't be staying home, but I couldn't bear to be alone either. . . .

And yet she felt that she wasn't being entirely selfish in accepting Dallas's offer to stay home with her this year. She knew how much Dallas missed her father. To be absolutely honest with herself, she had to admit that she had at times been jealous of the closeness between them, but now she thought their loss, hers and Dallas's, would bring them closer together. They would have this year to get to know each other better, to comfort each other. She had always hoped that as Dallas grew older they would become the close, intimate friends she imagined a mother and daughter should be. In so many ways Dallas was like her father, strong and outgoing, so different from Ellen herself, but Dallas often seemed a stranger. Ellen thought of Dallas as someone sure of herself in a way that she had never been, and certainly not when she was Dallas's age.

She did not think that depending on Dallas's strength was wrong. The one thing she had tried hard never to do was to put Dallas down, the way her mother had always been critical of her. She had never been able to please her mother. Even a few weeks ago, when she had called her mother in Florida to tell her of Hank's death, her mother had criticized her for not sending for her immediately. The scolding had left her with the same childish tears she had had in the past, and she had thought, I hope I never do that to Dallas. I hope Dallas will be my friend, my best friend.

Ellen stared out the window thinking, and her thoughts turned to Victor and Dallas. His quick, embarrassed confession of being in love made her smile, and then she realized, of course, Dallas had to be the one he was in love with. The thought gave her a stab of pain and made her feel old and terribly lonely. She mustn't be jealous of Dallas, her own daughter, and yet Dallas had everything ahead of her, while for her love was now all in the past. Still, she wasn't sure how Dallas felt. Was Dallas in love too, and was she jealous of the guitar lessons? Perhaps she should stop the lessons, but they gave her so much pleasure. . . .

Ellen buried her face in her hands, wanting to stop all thoughts, afraid of her own helplessness, aware as she was a hundred times a day of her inability to cope. She wanted to be a good mother to Dallas. She needed Dallas's love desperately. And yet she felt at this one time in her life she was entitled to indulge herself, not to have to please anyone, not her mother, not her daughter, and yes, not even Hank. She had had a miserable childhood and girlhood, hardly knowing her own father because he had traveled most of the time and always meeting criticism from her mother. And even with Hank, whom she had loved dearly, there had been adjustments to make: he wanted her to be social, to entertain, to share his passion for active sports, none of which she had ever been good at.

She had cared about his work. Her greatest pleasure had been when Hank turned to her for what he called her sharp eye for color. "You are better at that than I am," he had been fond of saying, and she would fill with pride. The thought gave her an idea.

She ran up to her bedroom and rummaged through a bureau drawer until she pulled out a bunch of fabric swatches. Before Hank had died she had planned to redo their bedroom, and now spread out on the bed before her were the samples of materials she had painstakingly gathered. She looked at them all and wondered what she'd had in mind. Carefully she examined them one by one, along with the color samples of paint and squares of wallpaper. They were a confused jumble. She tried to concentrate and remember why she had picked any of them, what colors were supposed to go with what, but the only result was that she felt dizzy and sick to her stomach. Feeling a compulsion to make a choice, she picked up a floral pattern for a bedspread and then put one solid wall color after another next to it, or perhaps a matching wallpaper for one wall and the others solid. But she could not make up her mind. What difference did any of it make? What was the use of a sparkling, new bedroom without Hank in it? And what frightened her most was that she could not decide. She had lost her sureness, lost that confident, sharp-eye Hank had admired so much.

Ellen dumped all the colorful samples into the wastebasket and sat down on the edge of the bed. She was afraid, afraid of herself, afraid to be alone. She wished Dallas would come home. At last she went downstairs and made herself a fresh cup of coffee, trying to steady her nerves. She forced herself to go to the phone, and she called up Hank's partner, a young man who had joined him only a year before.

Ellen got past the secretary and finally had Sam on the phone. "Sam, are you by any chance free for lunch?" she asked.

"I'm afraid not. I'm awfully sorry. I'm up to my neck. We sure miss Hank around here. Sorry, Ellen, I guess I shouldn't say that to you. How are you doing? You must come over and have dinner with us. I'll ask Jane to give you a ring and make a date. Take care."

He sounded busy, in a hurry, and she hardly knew Jane, his wife, and had not warmed to her when they'd met. Ellen hung up the phone with the tears streaming uncontrollably down

45

her face, feeling absolute and utter rejection. She knew the reaction was foolish, illogical — there was no reason why he shouldn't be busy for lunch, be busy altogether — yet the rushed telephone conversation was the last straw in a day whose only remotely bright spot had been the guitar lesson with Victor. She didn't want to have dinner with Sam and Jane; she had wanted to see Sam, to talk about his work, to have that small connection with Hank. She wanted to be reminded that she'd been the wife of a fine architect, a woman who had been loved, not someone floundering alone, unable to pick out a color for a bedspread, who didn't even care whether she had a bedspread or not.

Ellen couldn't bear being alone in the house another minute, and she got up, put on her coat, and went out to the car. Without stopping to think, she knew where she wanted to go: the cemetery. She wanted to be close to Hank, to sit by his grave and hope to get some comfort from the simple, physical act of being there. She was there for a long while. At one point she pulled out some weeds, and then she went across the street to a nursery where she bought some plants and put them into the ground. Mostly she just sat. Her thoughts roamed over the years of her marriage, back to the time when she first went out with Hank, their excitement when she learned that she was pregnant, the vacation trips they had taken together. She kept trying to pull her

46

mind back to the present, to think some positive thoughts about a future, but all she kept drawing was a dull blank — except for the guitar lessons. They seemed the one, tiny light on her horizon. Yet she made a resolution before she left the cemetery: she was going to try to see their old friends. She was not going to be thrown by one rejection. Ellen comforted herself with the thought that, no matter what, she had Dallas and her young friends. That companionship was more than some widows had.

Ellen stopped at her friend Vi's house on the way home. She got a warm welcome. "I'm glad to see you!" Vi greeted her with a hug and a kiss. "Where've you been hiding? I hear about you, of course, from Vic. He goes around strumming that guitar, and he thinks you're terrific. Have a cup of coffee. . . ."

"Victor's very good. He was a dear to suggest those lessons. They've been wonderful for me. I have two new pupils coming this week. Nancy and a friend of hers."

Later, as both women sat drinking their coffee, Vi asked, "How's it been going for you, Ellen? I worry about you. No one sees you; no one hears from you. You shouldn't be alone so much."

"I'm not alone. I have Dallas, and her friends are around a lot. It's nice to have the house filled with kids."

"I know, but. . . ." Vi was looking at her

with a worried expression on her face. "I'm going to talk to you straight. We're old friends so why not? Having kids around is great, but they're not your life. You can't depend on kids, on Dallas and her friends. You've got to make your own life."

Ellen thought of Sam's impatient voice on the phone, but she didn't want to act the complaining widow to Vi. "I'm not depending on them; I simply feel more comfortable with the kids. You can't understand — no one can — until it happens. You're all couples, and I'm not part of your life anymore. I don't have the same problems as the rest of you. You and I can't talk about the things we used to, about our husbands, their careers, our marriage."

Vi stretched out her hand to Ellen. "I know it's hard, believe me I do. But we all care about you. You're still you, an attractive woman with lots to talk about, a lot to offer. This is when you need your friends, what friends are for. Why don't you invite a few people over for dinner, the way you and Hank used to? I'll help you. Maybe in your own home it will be better than going to someone else's. Hank would like it, Ellen."

Ellen didn't want to cry, but the tears were choking her throat. "Hank's dead, and I have to go on living. It isn't fair . . . it just isn't fair. . . ." Vi put her arms around her until she stopped sobbing. ". . . I'm sorry. I feel okay

48

one minute, and the next I burst into tears. I'll try. I'll give a little dinner party. . . ." But she knew that her heart wasn't in it. She felt like a child obediently doing what her mother tells her to do as she sat making plans with Vi for a small dinner party.

She was just about to leave when Victor came home.

"Hey, I'll walk back with you and get my guitar," he said.

"Good." Ellen had to walk quickly to keep up with Victor's long stride, and her full skirt was blowing up high around her legs. A laundry truck went by, and the driver let out a loud whistle. Ellen looked around to see who was his target.

Victor laughed. "He was whistling at you. Doesn't that make you feel good?"

"It's ridiculous. I'm not a kid."

"You look like one."

Ellen saw that he wasn't teasing her. "Sometimes I feel like one. Say, when you were little, did you ever play that you couldn't walk on the lines on the sidewalk? We used to do that. Like this." Ellen started to walk carefully, avoiding the lines and the cracks. In a few seconds Victor was following her. They were both giggling as they progressed. Once Ellen had to take a wide jump and almost fell, but Victor caught her in time.

When they reached the Davis house, Ellen

sighed. "That was fun. I didn't think I would ever laugh again. Thanks, Victor."

"Anytime. At your service."

Dallas was in the kitchen when they came into the house. Her hello was cool, and Ellen's sudden burst of good spirits left her. What was she laughing about? Nothing had changed. For her the house was still empty, and Dallas's coolness was too much for her to cope with. She craved warmth and affection, longed physically for Hank, for his comforting arms, his warm smile. She wanted to cry with angry, bitter tears because the tiny bit of warmth that a mere kid like Victor gave her could mean so much. Being so dependent on such tiny crumbs was frightening.

"Victor, why don't you stay for supper?" she asked, thinking he would cheer Dallas up.

"There's not much to eat," Dallas said. "I was just going to fry an egg for myself."

"Well, don't. Vic, call up Vi and tell her you'll have supper here. I'll take a steak out of the freezer, and we can have a bottle of wine. We'll have a party, just the three of us." Ellen felt desperate. The whole house suddenly seemed hostile to her, and she was afraid that if she was alone with Dallas she would start crying hysterically.

"Sounds good," Victor said, and made for the phone in the hall.

Ellen went over to Dallas and put her arms

around her. "Are you all right? You'd like Victor to stay, wouldn't you?" She could feel Dallas stand rigid and still in her arms. "Dallas, please Dallas, don't turn against me. What am I doing that's wrong? I need you now so much. Maybe that's wrong, but bear with me, just for a while, please. . . ."

Then Dallas was sobbing wildly and pushing herself free. "Don't you ever think that I miss my father too? You're not the only one who's had a loss. I'm not some rock for you to lean on. I have moods and feelings too. I loved my father more than anyone in the world. . . ." And she ran out of the room.

In her mind Ellen finished the sentence for her, ". . . more than I ever loved you." Ellen felt numb. She was still standing there, not even thinking, in a state of shock when Victor came back into the room.

"What's the matter? Where's Dallas?"

"I think she's gone up to her room." Ellen was surprised by the calmness of her voice. "Why don't you go up to her? I'll get dinner started."

Victor looked puzzled, but she could hear him leaping the stairs, calling, "Dallas, you up there?"

Mechanically Ellen started preparations for dinner. She took the steak out and set the table. Only when she got out the bottle of wine from the leather wine holder on the wall did she burst into tears. She and Hank had bought the leather holder together on one of their vacations. It had been handmade in a little shop in a Maine waterfront town where they had climbed rocks together and gone fishing and had a glorious time.

Ellen had lost her appetite for food, but she still wanted terribly for dinner to be a party. If her mother had ever invited a boyfriend of hers for dinner, she'd have thought the millenium had come. Her mother had always criticized her friends; they had never been welcome in her house. Ellen wanted desperately to make life different for Dallas. Before, Hank had brought gaiety into the house, and now she didn't want Dallas to be stuck home alone with a mournful, silent mother. The most important thing she could do now, she believed, was to keep the house filled with cheerful young people, to keep both their lives as full of fun as possible.

"Dallas, Victor, are you coming down? I'm going to put the steak on. It'll take a while to cook because it's still frozen, but come down soon. Please," she called.

5

Dallas heard Victor loping up the stairs and calling her name, but she didn't answer him. At that moment she wished that both he and her mother would disappear and leave her alone. Her mother went around the house doing everything the way her father liked it — just the other day she had scolded Dallas for taking some books out of his study and not putting them back, as if it mattered — but Dallas was the one who had been made to betray him by not going to college. Dallas thought she'd never stop crying, and she didn't care. They were tears not only of grief, but of anger and bewilderment. How could you feel sorry for someone and almost hate her at the same time?

Sometimes I don't love my mother, I think. Sometimes I even hate her, Dallas thought, frightened by the vehemence she felt.

"I don't want any supper," she said to Victor, who was standing at her open door.

"What's the matter with you?"

"Nothing." Dallas spoke sullenly.

"Nuts." Victor came into the room and sat down on the bed beside her. He tried to put his arm around her, but she pushed him off. "Don't do that. Didn't you mean any of the things you said that night out in the hammock?"

Dallas spoke with her head muffled in a pillow. "I guess I meant them then."

Victor pulled her around so that she faced him. "You mean only then? What's happened to change you?" His face was deadly serious.

"I don't know. Nothing, I guess. Forget it."

"Forget what? That time in the hammock or now?"

"I don't know. Please, leave me alone. Go downstairs and have supper with Mom. She's calling."

"Are you mad because she invited me to stay? But that doesn't make any sense."

"Nothing makes any sense. It didn't make sense that my father died, it didn't make sense for me to stay home, it doesn't make any sense for my mother to think I'm her best friend. I'm not. I'm not a good person, Victor, so just forget about me."

"Don't say that. You're terrific to have stayed home this year. Not that I'm sorry," he added with a little grin, "but I know it must be hard to have your mother breathing down your neck every minute. Remember what we said that night. We love each other, Dallas, just hang on to that. That's what I do. When I get depressed about my lousy job, and I feel I'm just marking time, I think of you. It gives me a goal. I'm saving money, and my father says that in another year, when Andy's finished college, he can help me. Then I can get started to be a lab technician. Come on down. We can't let that steak and wine go to waste."

He put his arms around her again, and this time she nestled against his chest. When she looked up at him she had a half smile on her face. "I do love you, Vic, but everything gets so complicated."

"Tell me. You can talk to me."

"I know I can, about almost everything. But I get so mixed up about my mother, I can't even think straight. One minute she says she's depending on me too much, and I think, hurrah, she's going to stop. Then the next minute she doesn't want me out of her sight. The fact that she realizes what she's doing almost makes it worse. She doesn't seem to have any control."

Victor was sympathetic. "Maybe she hasn't. Maybe that's the trouble."

"I know. But that's pretty awful, isn't it?"

Victor took her in his arms, and she let him hold her close. "She'll get better," Victor said. "My mother said it takes time."

When Dallas came downstairs, she resolved not to let herself feel angry with her mother. Her mother's face looked particularly strained, and Dallas started to talk gaily. Soon the three of them were laughing. Dallas and her mother vied with each other in remembering funny things that had happened. "And how about the time I dropped the platter of spaghetti, smothered in meat sauce, right on the patio?" Dallas said, giggling.

"Not once, but twice, Victor. I couldn't believe it. She was about nine years old and insisted she could carry out the platter. But plop, down it went a second time."

"Anyway it wasn't as bad as when you spilled the chocolate milk all over your new white rug. You were crying and laughing at the same time," Dallas said.

"The funniest of all was when Dad and I were going to some big architects' shindig. Hank got all dressed up in his tuxedo and discovered the cleaner had sent him the wrong suit. The pants were about six inches above his ankles, and the sleeves were almost up to his elbows. He looked so funny, I laughed so hard, and he was so mad at the cleaner. Hank was furious with me for laughing until he saw

56

himself in the mirror, and then he couldn't stop laughing himself." Mrs. Davis was giggling now too.

"What did you do?" Victor asked.

"We had a terrible time. The cleaner was closed, and we had to find out where he lived. We finally did, I don't remember how, and it turned out that the mayor had Hank's suit. What a night that was! Fortunately the mayor was home and the cleaner got the suit from him and brought it over to us. We got where we were going just in time for salad and dessert, which Dad said was probably the only decent part of the meal anyway."

"I don't remember any of that," Dallas said.

"I guess you were too little," her mother said, wiping tears of laughter from her eyes. "I haven't laughed this much in a long time."

"I'm glad you can," Dallas said, feeling close to her mother and thinking that she had been imagining a lot of nonsense. It was a happy evening, and by the end of it Dallas was sure that her own emotional state had been the cause of her resentment of her mother.

"Wow, you're going to have some party," Dallas said to her mother and Vi Waters, sniffing the cooking smells in the kitchen. "Save some of that food for me."

Her mother looked up from the cutting board, where she was chopping vegetables.

"Why? Where will you be? You'll be home, won't you?"

"No, thanks. I don't want to be around for a dinner party. There's a group playing we all want to hear."

Her mother's face was distressed. "I took for granted you'd be home. I thought we'd be doing this together."

"I don't know where you got that idea. Vi's here to help you, and you'll have your friends." Dallas was on the run, half out the door, but her mother was still talking.

"Don't go off in such a rush," her mother said. "I thought you'd be a hostess with me. I suppose it sounds silly to you, but it's my first attempt at a dinner party without Hank, and I guess I'm nervous about it."

"It never occurred to me you'd want me home. You'll be okay. You've got to start sometime, Mom." Dallas knew her voice was getting impatient.

"Maybe I'm not ready yet. Oh dear. . . ." Her mother's voice trailed off, and she looked to Vi for help.

"You don't really need her," Vi said hesitantly. "We're in good shape."

Her mother's disappointment was written on her face. "It isn't a question of needing her. I guess I thought she'd want to be here, that she'd understand it was going to be a painful night for me."

"I'm sorry, Mom. I thought this party was supposed to be fun for you. Anyway I've arranged to go hear the group. They're playing only this one night. Besides what would I do with all your friends? I thought the whole idea was to —" she stopped short.

"Was to what?" her mother asked sharply.

Dallas felt embarrassed. "Was to get you together with your friends again. You know what I mean."

"It wasn't my idea. You and Vi persuaded me to do it. Now you won't even be here. I don't think it's very considerate."

"It's going to be fine," Vi said soothingly. "Everyone who's coming is an old friend. You don't have to be nervous."

"I don't have to be, but I am. I never was the one to give parties. Hank was the one. He made them work. I'm no good at it; I don't like being a hostess. I really counted on Dallas.

"Then you counted wrong." The minute the harsh words were out, Dallas felt guilty, but she stood her ground. The idea had truly never occurred to her to stay home for her mother's party, and she had thought it lucky that the group was playing that same night, so she could get out without leaving her mother alone. She said as much to her mother. "It's the first time I've gone out since Dad died, and you won't be alone, so you should be glad," she ended up.

"I can't force you to stay home, but it would be nice," her mother said lamely.

Dallas walked out of the house. She had been headed for the library, but instead she took the path up into the woods. She walked up to her fallen tree and sat down. The last time she'd been here was the day her father died, and all her feelings of loss came flooding back. What would her mother do if she just packed up and left? she wondered. But she couldn't do that; she knew she couldn't. Leaving would be a betrayal of her father. But what *was* she to do? Was a seventeen-year-old girl supposed to take care of her mother? To be a companion to her constantly? Dallas had read enough books to know that in the Victorian age many unmarried spinsters (and a woman was a spinster then if she wasn't married in her early twenties) had been stuck at home taking care of aging parents, and there was sixty-year-old Miss Jackson and her ninety-year-old mother right in Millstone. But not me, Dallas vowed to herself fervently. Not me.

Yet what was she to do? Dallas's sense of loss was turning to anger and resentment. She wanted to stand up and shout, "Get off my back, Mom, get off my back!"

While Dallas knew that her mother had depended heavily on her father, she didn't believe that her mother had to be as helpless as she now was. She's not even trying — she's depending on me for everything, for her life — and I can't bear it, I can't bear it. . . . Dallas choked back her sobs. She didn't want to cry; she wanted to think. She wanted to figure a way out of her dilemma, but she could find no answer. It's going to go on and on, she thought, until I'm an old lady and it'll be too late for anything. Sometimes I hate my mother, I hate her, I hate her. . . .

At last Dallas got up and went on to the library. She met Jennifer there, and after the girls had picked out their books they stopped for a soda.

"I'm glad you're getting out tonight," Jen said.

"Me too. You'd better believe it."

"It must be awful having to stay home all the time." Jennifer was sipping her soda thoughtfully.

"At least the kids come over. That's a help."

Jennifer gave her a sidelong glance. "Don't count on it forever."

Dallas could tell that Jennifer had something on her mind. "What's the matter? Tell me."

Jennifer looked uneasy. "Well, it's not much fun with your mother around. I mean, we really want to help, but why does she sit there all the time?"

"She likes young people," Dallas said flatly. Then she turned to her friend. "I don't blame the kids if they stop coming around, but then I'd never see anyone. I don't know what to do."

"Don't worry about it. I shouldn't have said anything. At least you're going out tonight. We'll still come over as much as we can. Sooner or later your mother will feel better, and she won't need you so much."

"I sure hope so."

When Dallas left Jennifer she was feeling more depressed than ever, but the thought of the evening cheered her up somewhat.

"You look beautiful." Dallas had come into her mother's room to say good-bye, and she was taken aback by her mother's good looks. Mrs. Davis was wearing a long, clingy dress that showed off her figure. Her long hair was brushed so that it was shiny and silky, it's gold color accentuated by long, gold earrings. "It's nice to see you all dressed up."

"I don't know what for. They say it's good for morale, but sometimes I think it can be more depressing when there's no one you care about dressing up for."

"Oh, Mother! There are lots of people. I care."

Her mother gave her a halfhearted smile. "You're a dear, but it's not the same. You look very pretty yourself," she added.

Dallas had felt she looked okay in a long,

denim skirt and a sheer, white Indian blouse, but looking at herself in the mirror she felt that she couldn't touch her mother in looks. Her mother seemed to be reading her mind. "You're a very pretty girl, Dallas. More than pretty, you're beautiful. You have such vitality in your face, and your skin glows. You'll still be glowing when I'm old and wrinkled. Don't forget that."

"You'll never get old. I can't imagine you old."

"I will, though. We're a mutual admiration society," her mother added with a laugh. Then she said casually, "When will you be home?"

"I don't know. Probably late. Don't wait up for me."

"I never go to sleep until you're home — if I get to sleep at all."

"Maybe you should take a sleeping pill."

"I hate sleeping pills. Don't get home too late." An anxious note was creeping into her voice.

"Don't pin me down. Listen, Mom, I'm seventeen, going on eighteen, and I haven't been out in over two months now. Maybe your party will be late, and you'll be tired enough to sleep."

"I'm never sleepy after a party. The nicest part is always sitting in the kitchen afterward and talking about it. I'm disappointed you won't be here, but I thought when you came home you could tell me about your evening and I'd tell you about mine. It's awful not to have anyone to share something with. . . ."

Dallas was speechless. How could you tell your mother that you didn't want to share your life with her? Her mother was looking at her so appealingly, and even though she smiled she gave the impression that her tears were near the surface.

"You can tell me about it in the morning," Dallas said in a gentler voice. "Please don't wait up for me. It will make me nervous. I'm looking forward to tonight."

"I wish I were," her mother said glumly. "I'll be nervous worrying about you. You know it is a responsibility to bring up a teenage daughter without a father."

"Mom, you don't have to bring me up. I'm brought up. I'm not a little kid anymore. What do you think's going to happen to me? I'm not about to get pregnant or anything like that. Stop worrying."

"Don't talk that way. I don't like it. I worry about everything now more than I used to. I can't help it. The smallest thing throws me into a panic — paying the bills, making sure the oil gets delivered, having the furnace cleaned, so many things Hank automatically took care of. I don't want to have to sit up and worry about you too."

"You don't have to sit up and worry about me," Dallas yelled. She didn't mean to shout, but she did. "Dad's dying was terrible enough, but you're making it a tragedy every minute of the day. I miss Dad as much as you do, but he loved life and he would want us to. I don't think you want me to go out tonight because you don't *want* me to enjoy myself. That's the crux of it. You're ruining my life."

Her mother looked shocked. She stood still and stared at Dallas. When she spoke her words were slow and distinct as if each one was said with a great effort. "That's the worst thing anyone ever said to me."

"I'm sorry." Dallas felt guilty, but she also believed what she had said. "I don't want to fight with you. That's the last thing in the world I want. But you don't need to feel so responsible for me. I'm old enough to be responsible for myself."

"You think you are, but you're still very young."

Dallas shook her head impatiently. "I don't understand you. You want to be young and with kids, but you're the most old-fashioned mother I ever heard of. You think you're modern, but you're not. You're worse than a Victorian grandmother! You may look young, but you sure aren't."

"I think that's about enough," her mother said angrily. "I didn't want this party in the first place, and now you've about ruined it for me."

"I didn't mean to. You know I didn't. But

you didn't have to tell me when to come home either. I hope your party is good, I really do." Dallas went over to kiss her mother good-bye, and her mother gave her a cool kiss on the cheek.

Dallas felt terrible when she walked down the street to Jennifer's. Victor and Ted were going to pick the girls up there. She was angry with her mother, and at the same time upset about quarreling with her. Yet she had meant every word of what she had said. She felt that her mother *was* making their tragedy such a living part of their everyday lives that she was causing them to suffer much more than they had to.

The pub was crowded with Dallas's friends and many of the young people from the area, but Victor found a table for the four of them not too far from where the musicians would be playing. Dallas was anxious for the music to start. She didn't feel like talking and wanted only to sit back and listen to the music.

The music was good, and it suited Dallas's mood. She wanted to empty her mind, and the music did so for her. She let the sounds seep through her, so that she wasn't thinking at all, just listening. Sometimes she could feel Victor looking at her, studying her face, but he had the sense not to talk, which she appreciated. The music stopped at one o'clock, and then they went to an all-night diner, where they stuffed themselves with grinders.

It was around two thirty in the morning when Victor drove her home. Dallas was alarmed to see her house lit up like a Christmas tree. She ran inside, with Victor close behind her, and found her mother, wrapped in a robe, pacing the floor. "Thank God you're home. Where have you been?"

"At the pub, and then we stopped for something to eat. What's the matter? What happened?" Dallas was frightened by her mother's pale, strained face.

"What's the matter!" her mother shrieked. "What do you think's the matter? It's half past two. I've been waiting for you since midnight. I've been worried sick."

"I told you not to wait up for me," Dallas said. "How was your party?"

"Terrible. I couldn't wait for them to go home. I knew it wouldn't work, and it didn't."

"You didn't want it to work. You made up your mind before that it wouldn't. What went wrong?"

"Everything. I couldn't stand it. Everyone feeling sorry for me, having them here without Hank. It was ghastly. I felt like an outcast, listening to their plans for vacation trips over the holidays, everyone in couples, no one who *really* cared about me. It's no use. . . ."

"Mom, they do care. You just think they don't. It's all in your mind."

"Wherever it is, it's there. I can't help it. It's the way I feel. I'm sorry, Victor, to talk this way in front of you, but I think you understand better than my own daughter does."

That remark made Dallas boil with anger. "That's a terrible thing to say."

"I think you're just upset, Ellen," Victor said. "Why don't you put on a coat, and we'll all go for a little ride and cool off? It'll make you sleepy," he added.

Mrs. Davis's face brightened. "That's a great idea." She went to get her coat.

"You can go for a ride," Dallas said to Victor. "I'm going to bed."

"Come on, please. It will calm your mother down."

"Right now I don't care whether she calms down or not. She's not the only one who's missing my father, and I can't take much more of this."

"Dallas, please come." Victor's face was pleading. "I don't want to go for a ride with your mother. I was just trying to be helpful."

Dallas shook her head. "No. I'm afraid you're stuck with her. I'm sorry, Vic, but I just don't want to go."

"Damn, I guess I *am* stuck. Damn. It was a nutty suggestion."

"Okay, kids, I'm ready. Let's go." Her mother sounded more cheerful.

"I'm going to bed. Good night," Dallas said.

"Dallas, please come," her mother asked.

"I don't feel like it. Good night."

Up in her room Dallas could hear Victor start up the motor and the car take off. Then the situation of her mother off riding with her boyfriend at three o'clock in the morning struck her as funny, but in a hurtful, angry way. What would her father have made of it? But none of this would be happening if he were alive, Dallas thought. The whole world wouldn't be turning upside down; her mother wouldn't be going crazy. She banged her fist against her pillow in anger, and then, exhausted, buried her head in the pillow and fell asleep.

She was awakened by a sound and realized it was the car coming into their driveway. Then she heard her mother opening and closing the front door. Dallas peered at her night clock and saw that it was after four o'clock. I hope they had a good time, she thought ruefully, and turned her face back into the pillow. This time, however, she didn't fall asleep for a long time. She was adding figures in her head: Victor was eighteen and a half, and her mother was thirty-seven. She had heard and read about young men falling in love with older women, but she wondered if older women also fell in love with young men. The thought made her sick, and she tried to think of something else so that she could get to sleep.

6

The next morning Dallas and her mother had a late breakfast. Mrs. Davis seemed in a good mood. "I guess going to bed late is the trick," she said. "At least last night when I got to bed I fell asleep."

"That's good. Maybe you should go out riding every night," Dallas suggested.

Her mother gave her a sharp look. "Victor's a very nice boy. Vi and I used to talk about you two when you were little. We always thought how nice it would be if you and he got together. Vi would be a good mother-in-law."

"If you don't mind, I'll pick my own mother-in-law. Or perhaps I should say my own husband — if I ever do."

"Of course." Dallas could tell that her mother was determined to keep things smooth. "But you can't blame me for noticing, and for hoping too."

"You can hope all you want, but it won't do you any good. I told you before I don't want to discuss Victor with you."

"You don't want to discuss anything with me." The determination was rapidly weakening.

"That's right. I don't. I don't want to discuss my friends." And I don't want to share them either, Dallas added to herself. She had a strong feeling that her mother was ruining everything between Victor and herself. She didn't know exactly why, but her mother's approval of Victor irked Dallas to the point of making her want to turn against him. Her mother treated Victor as if he were already one of the family, as if he somehow belonged to her as much as to Dallas. Dallas couldn't stand the way her mother overreacted to Victor's attentions. She should realize that Victor was trying to be helpful mainly because of Dallas. But Dallas felt impatient with Victor too, because he played up to her mother and did dumb things like suggesting the ride the night before.

Dallas felt out of sorts with everyone. She was sick of staying home, tired of hanging around. She didn't often indulge in self-pity, but today she felt that her life was truly a mess. Victor was the one good thing in it, and she felt that her mother was nibbling away at the relationship. Logically or not she was annoyed with Victor too. Some part of her wanted Victor to be the one to get her mother off her back since she seemed incapable of doing so herself, although she knew that no one could make the break for her.

Dallas still had these thoughts on her mind when Victor came by later in the afternoon for his guitar lesson. He was there early, and her mother was out at the beauty parlor getting her hair done.

"Is your mother feeling better today?" Victor asked, after he had greeted Dallas and there had been a dead silence for several minutes.

"Of course. Riding with you last night was fantastic."

"You should have come with us."

Dallas glanced across the kitchen table, where they were having a soda, to look at Victor. She took a sip before answering. "Riding around with my mother at three o'clock in the morning is not my idea of fun."

"It's not mine either. I only suggested it because I thought you were coming along."

"Well, you thought wrong." Dallas spoke firmly, and stood up to take her empty glass to the sink.

Victor got up too and tried to put his arms around her, but Dallas pushed him away. "What's eating you?" he demanded. "You're the one who changes every minute. Don't take your problems with your mother out on me. Dammit, I think you're jealous of her."

Dallas whirled around to face him. "Don't be stupid. What's there to be jealous of? I think she's acting ridiculously, and you're helping her make a fool of herself."

"What the hell have I done?" Victor looked truly surprised.

"If you don't know, I can't tell you. Forget it."

"You're always telling me to forget it. I don't want to. You can at least tell me what I do that's wrong." Victor was facing her with his hands on her arms.

"I feel sorry for my mother," Dallas said, speaking slowly, searching for the right words. "But I think she's relying too much on us, on you and me and the kids, instead of facing her own life. And I don't want to encourage her."

"And you think I have?"

Dallas nodded. "I don't really blame you. My mother's crazy about you, but —"

"But you don't like it," Victor finished for her.

"No, I don't," Dallas said vehemently.

"Well, I think you've got a pretty wild

imagination. And I think you *are* jealous of your mother."

"If that's what you think, think it," Dallas said angrily.

"I've been trying to be nice to your mother because of what happened, but mainly because of you, you dumb idiot. I thought you'd like me to. And I think it's too damn bad that you don't."

"Well, bully for you. Here's my mother now," Dallas said, as the car pulled into the driveway. "You can have your guitar lesson."

"I certainly will."

Dallas slammed out of the kitchen and went up to her room.

She certainly made a mess of that, she decided, aware again that in some far-out fantasy she wanted Victor to solve her problem for her. She was furious with herself for feeling so helpless, unreasonably annoyed with Victor because he was absolutely right to be nice to her mother (though in her fantasy he told her off), and most of all angry with her mother. Her mother was at the bottom of all the trouble, behaving the way she did, as if she hadn't a friend of her own in the world, as if she were the only woman who had ever been widowed. Dallas felt a deep, anguished longing for her father. He would understand, but then, of course, if he were alive none of this would have happened.

She was sitting and brooding, half listening

to the guitars playing downstairs and to her mother's and Victor's voices, when the phone rang. It was Jennifer, and Dallas agreed to go over to her house. "I suppose I can go out now. My mother has Victor here," she said.

In a few minutes she was at Jen's house, and Jen suggested that they go for a walk. Jen had no classes and had some shopping she wanted to do. "Have you heard the news?" Jen asked, when they were outside.

"No, what?"

"Andy Waters is coming home from college."

Dallas was surprised. "I just saw Victor, and he didn't say anything. I guess he didn't have a chance. We had a fight. Tell me about Andy first, and I'll tell you about Victor later."

"I saw Mrs. Waters this morning, and I think she's pretty upset. Andy is tired of school and decided to take a year off. She'll be furious if he doesn't get his tuition back, but he said he was sure he would because it's still early in the term."

"What's he going to do?"

"He wants to stay home and write, she said. I bet he'll never finish college. He waited a year to go, didn't he?"

"Yes, he did. He must be twenty-two or -three by now."

"What did you and Victor fight about?" Jennifer asked.

Dallas's mind was spinning ahead, wondering what Andy's being home would mean for Victor. Would there be money for him to go to school sooner? But she answered Jennifer's question.

"It was stupid." Dallas told her about the night before and her mother's going out for a ride with Victor. "I certainly wasn't going to go with them," she ended up. "The whole thing was crazy."

"What are you going to do, Dallas? Maybe you ought to look for a job," Jennifer suggested.

"Doing what? I don't want to be a baby-sitter, and I hate housework. What's there to do around here for someone like me? Besides I bet my mother wouldn't let me."

"But what are you going to do?"

"Sweat out this year and go to college next year, I hope. If she lets me. Maybe I'll never get away. I keep thinking I'll figure out something, but so far I haven't had any brain-storms."

They had walked to a shopping plaza, and Jennifer said she wanted to buy some slacks. The girls discovered that a sale was on, and since Dallas knew her mother had a charge account at the store, she picked out a pair of slacks too. The girls were delighted with their purchases and wandered around looking at other shops.

They stopped at a jeweler's, and both girls

became enchanted with the display of earrings. "Let's go in," Jennifer said.

There was a large assortment, and the girls peered admiringly over display cases. The only trouble was that most of the earrings, and particularly those that they liked, were made for pierced ears. "Why don't you girls get your ears pierced?" the woman behind the counter suggested. "It takes only a few minutes, and it doesn't hurt, I promise you. It's just a little pinprick."

"Maybe I'll buy some earrings and get my ears pierced later," Jennifer said.

The saleswoman shook her head. "That's not the way to do it. You couldn't try them on, and earrings look different when they're on. I wouldn't like to sell them to you that way."

"Let's do it," Dallas said. "Let's get them pierced."

The girls looked at each other and giggled. "Why not?"

The price that the saleswoman quoted them didn't seem too much, and it included the tiny gold earrings the girls would have to wear after their ears were pierced.

"But I don't have any money with me now," Dallas said.

"Neither do I," Jennifer added.

"Actually my partner, who does the piercing, isn't here right now. She'll be back in an hour or so. Why don't you girls go home, get your money, and come back in around an hour and a half? And don't get cold feet," she added, as the girls agreed and were leaving. "You'll be glad to have it done."

Dallas was enthusiastic as they walked across the plaza toward home. "I adore earrings, but I keep losing the screw-on ones. I've been wanting to do this for ages, but I never had the courage. Victor will be happy. He says my earrings are always falling off. Aren't you excited?"

Jennifer nodded. "Sure, but I hope it doesn't hurt."

"She said it wouldn't. Let's get a slice of pizza. You want to?"

"Yes, I'm starving."

They got their slices and ate them as they continued their walk slowly. The day, which had been cloudy earlier, had cleared up into beautiful fall sunshine. Dallas gave a contented sigh. "This has been the best couple of hours I've had in a long time." She put her arm through Jennifer's. "Not that we've done anything spectacular, but I was able to get away from home, and . . . ." She hesitated, and didn't finish her sentence.

"And get away from your mother," Jennifer finished for her.

Dallas smiled wryly. "I didn't want to say so, but it's true. She makes me feel so heavy.

She's around all the time, trying to live her life in mine. Now she's taken over Victor, and she's kind of killing everything between us. I should be glad that she likes him, but she's so possessive. You know, I wish she'd meet a man and get married again."

"It's much too soon. But maybe she will one day. She's still young, and she's pretty."

"She'll never meet anyone hanging out with us. And I can't imagine having a stepfather either. That might be worse." Dallas stopped to throw her pizza-stained paper napkin into a trash bin. "I shouldn't talk this way."

"It's okay," Jennifer said. "It's only me."

Victor had left by the time the girls got to Dallas's house. The minute Dallas walked inside, she knew, before her mother said a word, that her mother had been waiting for her and wondering where she was. Dallas didn't give her mother a chance to say anything but immediately opened her package to show the slacks. "They were on sale. Aren't they terrific? They fit just right. I know you'd be glad I bought them. And Mom, Jen and I are going back to have our ears pierced. We saw the most adorable earrings, so many I hardly know which to pick, and they're not expensive. They have loads of them for two and three dollars."

Jennifer showed Mrs. Davis her purchases too. "You girls sound excited. You really had a good time," Mrs. Davis said. "Why didn't you wait for me? I would have loved to have gone with you. Anyway I'll go back with you and get my ears done too. I've always wanted to. What fun! We can go to the pub for supper too. Wouldn't that be nice, just the three of us?"

Dallas could feel her chest tightening, and her mind searched wildly for an excuse not to go. "We may not have time to get our ears done now. Jen and I were planning to go to a movie." She knew the minute she'd spoken that she had said the wrong thing, and she looked at Jennifer hopefully.

Jennifer looked surprised, but before she could answer, Mrs. Davis spoke up. "We can do everything. We can get our ears done, have supper, and go to the eight o'clock show. What movie were you going to?"

"I forget the name of it," Dallas said helplessly. She knew she was licked.

Mrs. Davis shrugged. "I don't care what we see, whatever you girls want. Oh, this will be fun. I was dreading another empty evening at home. There's not even anything to watch on TV tonight." She hugged Dallas. "I don't know what I'd do without you. I'll go upstairs and get out of these old slacks and be down in a minute."

Dallas looked at Jennifer helplessly. "You see what I mean?"

Jennifer was laughing. "I know I shouldn't

laugh — it *is* pretty awful — but your face when your mother said she was coming with us was really funny. You never should have said we were going to a movie."

"I know. But I couldn't think of a darn thing we could do that she wouldn't do with us. There isn't anything," she added gloomily. "And when she hugs me and says she couldn't get along without me, it's worse. I should write a song, 'Sometimes I Don't Love My Mother, I Think.' It keeps running through my head."

"I guess we all don't love our mothers sometimes. Maybe mothers don't love us either."

"I wish my mother didn't love me so much," Dallas said.

Her mother came downstairs in a short while, looking very chic in a camel-colored pants suit. "You're all dressed up," Dallas said.

"Why not? It's a treat for me to go out with you two."

Dallas had no answer. She no longer wanted to get her ears pierced, she didn't want to go to the movies, she didn't want to have supper out with her mother. She and Jennifer had been having a good time together, but now everything had gone flat. She wanted to be a good sport, and her mother's enthusiasm was sad and touching, but going out with Jennifer and going out with her mother and Jennifer were two different things.

Dallas tried hard. They all had their ears

pierced — it *was* like a pinprick and took only a few seconds — and they all got mimeographed sheets of instructions on how to take care of their ears until they were healed. After they selected earrings, though, there was little to talk about. Alone, Dallas and Jennifer never ran out of conversation, but during supper there were long silences that her mother tried to fill with a lecture about nutrition. Since her husband's death, Mrs. Davis had become very concerned about food and diet, and she tried hard to persuade the girls not to order pizzas. Dallas didn't dare tell her that they each had already had a slice in the afternoon. "Did you ever read the list of ingredients that go into these things?" Mrs. Davis demanded.

"Those are frozen. These aren't," Dallas said patiently.

"I don't think there's much difference," her mother said. "There's no nutritional value in them, just a lot of unhealthy fat."

"Mom, you're the one who wanted to go out for supper. You eat what you want and let me eat what I want."

"After what happened to your father, Dallas. . . ."

"Please, Mom. Let's not talk about it now."

Her mother's hurt look made Dallas feel both guilty and terribly depressed. Her mother could never seem to let go of her pain for a moment. She not only had to carry it with her constantly, she had to take it out and examine it for others to see. Dallas kept telling herself that not quite three months had gone by since her father had died, and she was being impatient with her mother, but when, when was she going to start to face her new life?

After the movie, when they had taken Jennifer home and were back in their own house, Dallas could see that her mother wanted to sit up and talk. Dallas wanted to go to bed, but, trying to be as nice as she could, she sat down at the kitchen table with her and drank a glass of milk she didn't want.

"Jennifer is such a nice girl," her mother said. "You do have nice friends, Dallas. You're very lucky, and I'm happy for you."

"You have nice friends too. Vi would do anything for you. And what about the people you and Dad saw all the time, the Burnses and the Dugans and the Bernsteins?"

Mrs. Davis wrinkled her nose. "I know. They're all very nice people. I have nothing against them. But I just don't feel right with them anymore."

"But what will you do if I go away to college next year? I probably shouldn't talk about it now, but you know how much Dad wanted me to go to college, and I want to go too. You'd be alone so much . . . ."

"I've been considering next year, darling.

Don't think I don't appreciate what you're doing, staying home this year with me. You should go to college, and I'd like to see you with a profession of your own. But perhaps a school in a city would be better for you. I know you fell in love with New Hampshire, but outside of the school there's nothing there, no cultural life. I thought if you went to a school, say, in Boston, I wouldn't mind getting out of here for a change too. We could take a little apartment together. It would be no more expensive than a dorm, probably cheaper, and being in a city could be fun. We could go to concerts and the theater. I might even take some courses myself."

Dallas listened to her mother with her heart dropping as she talked. Oh, no, Dallas's mind was screaming, *no, no, no!* This suggestion was too much. The one gate ahead that she had seen open, the only gate in a solid, thick wall, was being gently, firmly closed in her face. Her mother was so logical, so enthusiastic, so buoyed up by her idea that Dallas could only look at her in amazement and keep her dismay to herself. If her mother were mean to her, if she picked on her the way some mothers did, if she openly tried to undermine her, she could get angry and fight back. Yet her mother didn't do any of those things. She just clung. She had always taken for granted that she loved her mother, but she had never felt her mother's dependency before. Naturally not. Her father had been there for her mother to hold on to, and Dallas hadn't paid much attention to their relationship. It had seemed okay that her father had made her parents' social life, that he had brought people and liveliness into the house, and that her mother had been content to let him do so.

"I don't know, Mom, I really did like New Hampshire, and so did Dad. We don't have to decide now, do we? There's lots of time."

"I like to think ahead, to have something to look forward to," her mother said wistfully. "My life seems so empty now, and when I think of the years stretching ahead, alone . . . ."

"Don't think that way," Dallas said. "You may not be alone."

"Widows are alone," her mother said dolefully.

They were still sitting in the kitchen when the telephone rang. It was after ten o'clock, and Dallas wondered who could be calling. She answered quickly. "It's Grandma calling from Florida," she said in an aside to her mother, before turning the phone over to her.

Dallas could hear her mother's end of the conversation: "I'm doing all right. . . . No, I'm not by myself. I have Dallas here. I told you she stayed home with me. . . . No, this wouldn't be a good time for you to come to visit. . . . The weather's not good now. . . .

Maybe in the spring. . . . No, Mom, I don't think you should come now. . . . No, I don't want to come to Florida. I have a lot of things to take care of, about the estate and all . . . . Thank you for calling, take care."

Her mother gave a long sigh when she hung up. "The last thing in the world I want now is my mother."

"Maybe a trip to Florida would be good for you," Dallas said.

Her mother scowled. "Not to visit my mother. She's not what I need right now. Too depressing. I'd be with a bunch of old ladies down there, and she upsets me."

Dallas stared moodily into her empty milk glass. How could she tell her mother that she felt the same way about her?

7

Dallas had been dreading Thanksgiving. She knew that her mother dreaded it too, and she could be honestly sympathetic with her. There was no use in asking any of her friends over, since they all would want to be home with their own families. And the idea of the two of them going to a restaurant alone was too depressing. Then Vi Waters invited them to dinner, and Dallas was greatly relieved when her mother accepted.

But in spite of the fact that they were going out to dinner later in the day, Dallas could see immediately at breakfast that her mother was feeling very low. "I would like to go to the cemetery today," her mother said. "Would you come with me?"

Dallas had not gone to the cemetery since the funeral. She had simply said, "I can't," to her mother's repeated request, and her mother had gone without her. But today she felt different. She felt that she had to help her mother in every way that she could, so, keeping her apprehensions to herself, she agreed. The day was raw and cold, and when Dallas got into the car with her mother, she thought she had never felt more depressed in her life. In a way the return was worse than the funeral itself. The shock had worn off, and now she felt only the pain of their loss, both her own and her mother's, plus the heavy burden of the last months of living with her mother.

Dallas had never walked through a cemetery before. At the funeral she hadn't looked at anything, but today she went slowly, stopping to read the tombstones. She recognized family names from the town, and a few times she was shocked to read of six-month-old infants and two- and three-year-old babies who had died.

Her mother was silent, obviously wrapped in her own thoughts as she walked beside her. When they got to her father's grave, Dallas helped her mother pull out some weeds, pick off dead flowers, and the two of them sat on a narrow stone bench. Neither of them spoke, and Dallas, for the first time, understood why her mother kept coming back here. There was a certain quiet and peacefulness, a sense of closeness to her father. There was no logical explanation for her feelings, yet Dallas was sure that her mother felt the same way. The sense of closeness extended to and included her mother. Dallas felt ashamed of the bad thoughts she had been thinking about her and vowed not to let them take over again.

In a burst of tenderness she did something that she had thought she would never do. "When we leave here," she said, speaking softly, "I want to take you someplace."

Her mother looked at her inquiringly. "I'll show you where Dad used to take me all the time," Dallas said. "You remember when Dad and I made a tree house one summer, ages ago? You got mad because we spent so much time there. Dad said that it was my private place, and he was only there to help me build it."

"Yes, I remember. I wasn't mad. I guess I was hurt at being excluded."

"I thought you might like to see it."

"Now? After all these years?" Her mother's face did not brighten as Dallas had hoped. But she said, "That's dear of you. Yes, I'd like to go."

Dallas felt stupid sitting on the dead tree branch with her mother. What crazy impulse had made her bring her mother up here? she wondered. What had she expected? She didn't know, but whatever it was, her mother was not responding. She couldn't blame her. After all, it was only a patch of woods, and her mother had none of the memories that Dallas connected with it. Perhaps her mother was remembering her own hurt. Dallas had never thought of her mother being excluded; she had only been happy to be there with her father.

"It's pretty here," her mother said politely, the way a person says thank you without meaning it. "It's nice that you had this with your father."

"He didn't come up here with me that much," Dallas said, wanting to comfort her mother. "I was here a lot alone."

They didn't sit there very long. "We should be going home to get dressed to go over to Vi's. I'm not sure I wouldn't be better off staying home," her mother said.

"No, you wouldn't be. That would be awful. It will be okay at the Waters'."

"I hope so." Her mother did not sound convinced.

"It's wonderful to have you here." Vi Waters greeted them warmly. The house was filled with the good smells of a traditional Thanksgiving dinner: turkey and sweet potatoes, apple and pumpkin pies. Through the open living-room door Dallas could see the large dining-room table set with Vi's best linen and silver. Mr. Waters' parents, an aunt of Vi's, and another couple, the Dugans, who were friends of her parents, were also there.

After saying hello to everyone, Dallas gravitated to Victor and Andy, who had been home for several weeks by now. The three young people sat together, Dallas and Victor each with a glass of white wine, while Andy sipped a cocktail like the others.

"What are you going to do here all year?" Dallas asked Andy.

"I don't know. Think, I guess. I got sick of school."

"Someone said you wanted to write."

Andy looked defensive. "I'm not broadcasting that. I may turn out nothing. I have some ideas."

Dallas's mother was not far away, and she came over to them. "Did I hear you say you wanted to write, Andy?" she asked.

Andy's restless eyes stopped for a few seconds on Mrs. Davis's face and then wandered off again. He was a bigger, stronger-looking version of his younger brother, with a thrust to his chin that indicated an aggressiveness, even an arrogance, that Victor did not have.

"No, you didn't," he said bluntly. "Your daughter said she heard a rumor."

Mrs. Davis laughed. "It's not a crime, you know. I've often thought about writing myself. I have lots of ideas for stories."

"Why don't you?" Victor asked.

"I guess I haven't the confidence. I need

someone to push me. Isn't that the way you feel?" she turned to Andy.

"No." He looked bored and turned away to get himself another drink.

Mrs. Davis handed him her glass. "I'll have one too, please. Another of the same."

Dallas had often heard her mother say that one drink made her feel dizzy. She had already had two, and Dallas worried what a third would do to her. Her mother's face was flushed, and her eyes bright, but Dallas did not think she should say anything to her.

When Andy handed her glass back to her, Mrs. Davis herself said, "This will really get me cock-eyed, but I don't care. It's the only way I can get through this day."

"Why not?" Victor said sympathetically. "It must be rough for her," he added in a low tone to Dallas.

"I don't think getting drunk is going to help," Dallas said to him.

Dallas watched her mother down her third drink and center all her attention on Andy. Mrs. Davis was leaning over talking to him without stopping. Andy was lolling back in his chair, listening to her, sipping his own drink, with an expression on his face that Dallas could not fathom. She couldn't make out whether he was amused, bored, or leading her on with some devious plan to shut her up when it suited him. At first Dallas was apprehensive for her mother. Andy always had been an enigma to her. Victor jokingly called him a schizo, because he could be friendly and nice one time and then act as if you weren't there the next. Then she began to get angry. Still, she was not her mother's keeper, and she tried to talk to Victor and to pay no attention to the conversation going on in the corner between her mother and Andy.

But she wasn't doing a good job of ignoring them. "What did you say?" she asked Victor, when she realized he had said something she had not been listening to.

"I said don't worry so much about your mother. She can take care of herself."

"I'm not so sure. I hope Andy doesn't give her another drink."

"I'll tell him not to," Victor said.

"No, you'd better not. My mother might get mad."

Dallas didn't know what to do. Her mother's voice was getting louder, and she felt that something embarrassing and terrible was going to happen. She looked around the room and caught Mrs. Water's eye, who obviously also was aware of Andy and Mrs. Davis in their corner. Vi stood up and said that dinner was almost ready, and why didn't they all go in and sit down at the table?

Dallas got up quickly with relief. However, in the dining room she saw her mother hastily change places with Vi's aunt so that she could sit next to Andy. And then Mr. Waters began to serve the wine.

That morning Dallas had really been looking forward to going to the Waters' for dinner with her mother. She had felt close to her, had decided that she had been unfair, and resolved that from now on she was going to be sympathetic and warm, not resentful. But now, watching her mother center all her attention on Andy, not even bothering to talk to anyone else, Dallas was becoming resentful all over again. She started to do some figuring in her head. Andy had lost time in high school with hepatitis, and he had waited a year after high school before going to college. He had to be twenty-three years old now; her mother was thirty-seven.

Dallas remembered that this was the second time she had done such figuring. Andy was closer in age to her mother than Victor, yet the idea of her mother falling for Andy was as repugnant as thinking of her and Victor. Andy, of all people. He was attractive, very attractive. Lots of girls she knew had had crushes on him, but Andy had always gone his own way. Maybe that was his charm. No one ever knew what Andy really thought about anyone, and while he was not rude he kept a certain distance that people wanted to get through. To get a compliment from Andy was worth a million from anyone else.

But her mother couldn't seriously be interested in Andy. Dallas decided she was nuts even to be thinking such thoughts. As hungry as she had been before, however, her taste for the marvelous food set before her was gone. She just nibbled at it.

"What's the matter, Dallas? You're not eating." Mrs. Waters was looking at her sympathetically. "Are you all right?"

"I'm fine, and the food is delicious. I guess I ate too many crackers before we sat down."

"She's mad at me." Her mother's voice shot across the table. "I can tell. She's been keeping an eye on me all day." Her mother was obviously drunk. "My daughter doesn't approve of me. My mother never approved of me, and now my daughter doesn't. That's pretty funny, isn't it? She thinks I'm ancient, old-fashioned. Don't you, Dallas? Don't you?" Her mother's voice was high and bordered on the hysterical.

Dallas knew her face must be a fiery red, and tears were smarting in her eyes. She didn't know what to do or say and was grateful to Vi Waters for taking over.

"All our kids think we're ancient, the same way we thought our parents were. I remember I thought my science teacher in high school was an old man, and then later I discovered he was only fifteen years older than I. It made a big difference when I was fifteen, but then one of my classmates married him when she was thirty and he was forty-five, and the difference didn't seem much at all."

But there was no stopping Ellen Davis. "Dallas, you didn't answer me. When I ask you a question, you should answer. We taught you manners, your father and I. Your dear, darling father —" Her voice broke. "He wouldn't like you to be rude to me, but he's not here, is he? You would be nice to me if he were here. . . . Answer my question, Dallas!" Her voice turned sharp.

"I don't remember it," Dallas mumbled, wanting to die.

"She doesn't remember it." Her mother laughed hysterically. "She doesn't remember it. . . ."

Dallas could feel Victor's hand on her arm. She didn't dare look around the table, but she could feel the weight of everyone's silence and embarrassment.

"Oh, God, she doesn't remember it. . . ." Her mother started to weep with loud, racking sobs, and in a second Mrs. Waters was by her side and taking her out of the room. Dallas got up quickly and followed them.

Her mother was in the bathroom being sick. Vi was holding her head, and Dallas stood by, feeling helpless. She was both sorry for her mother and embarrassed.

When the sickness was over, her mother sat on the edge of the bathtub with a peaked, wan face. "I'll take you home," Dallas said.

Mrs. Davis shook her head. "No, I don't want to spoil your dinner. I can take myself home."

As if she hasn't spoiled it already, Dallas thought. "I don't mind. I don't think you should drive."

"I'm perfectly capable of driving," Mrs. Davis said, pulling up her hunched shoulders. "But I'll walk anyway. I'll leave the car for you."

"If you want to go home, Andy can take you. But why don't you lie down here until you feel better?" Vi suggested.

"No. I'm sorry I've been such a nuisance. I shouldn't have wine on top of a cocktail. Hank always said I was a cheap date when it came to drinking. If Andy doesn't mind taking me home, that will be fine."

"He'll be glad to," his mother said.

Dallas thought that arrangement was about the worst she could think of. Vi did persuade her mother to lie down until Andy finished his dinner. Dallas hated to go back to the table, but she had no choice. Everyone asked after her mother, and after Dallas and Vi assured them that she was all right, the whole unpleasant episode was dropped. But not for Dallas.

She had resented her mother before, but now she was frightened. She felt that her mother was living on such a shaky emotional level that she might do anything. Dallas wished that her grandmother had come up from Florida, but she was afraid her mother would be furious if she called her. And consulting her grandparents, who called regularly from Oregon, didn't make such sense to her. What would they do? She couldn't see any point in getting them alarmed.

Andy finished his turkey, said that he would have his dessert later, and went off to take her mother home. Dallas longed to leave too, but her mother had made it clear that she didn't want her daughter to go with her. She was glad that Victor gave up trying to make any conversation with her. They finished their meal in silence, with Dallas half listening to the general conversation, and at last they all got up from the table.

"What do you want to do?" Victor asked.

"I don't know. Nothing. Go home I guess. Maybe Andy's waiting for me to get there." She was wondering why he had been gone so long.

"I doubt it. Andy doesn't wait around for anyone. Do you want to go to a movie?"

Dallas really wanted to go home, but she thought that if she went to a movie her mother might be asleep by the time she returned. She dreaded another scene with her.

"Okay, let's go to a movie. It's better than sitting around."

"Anything's better," Victor agreed.

When Dallas said good-bye to Vi, she was grateful for her breezy voice saying, "Don't worry about your mother. That can happen to the best of us." Still Dallas was glad to get out into the fresh air. Victor took her arm and tucked her hand into his coat pocket with his own as they walked to the movie house. "Don't take it so hard," he said. "You're not responsible for your mother."

"I know. But I never thought she would be this way. She didn't use to be. Do you think she'll ever get better?"

"I don't know. But you can't wait around to see. I haven't had a chance to talk to my father yet, but I'm hoping now that Andy's left school, maybe I can go next fall. Not wait another year. If Andy does want to go back, I don't think my father will pay for it. Andy will have to make it on his own. You know what that means?"

"No, what?"

Victor squeezed her hand. "It means you and I could get married in a year or so."

Dallas was stunned. She was sure she loved Victor, but marriage was something to think about for the remote future. The thought gave her a scary but warm feeling. "How do you figure that?" She held on tightly to Victor's hand.

99

"If our parents pay for our tuition at school, which they'd do anyhow, we could both work and handle the rest. Lots of other couples do."

"Wouldn't that be terrific." Then she let out a long sigh. "You know what my mother said the other day? She wants me to go to school in Boston and take an apartment with me. Maybe I'll never be able to get married. Maybe you'd have to marry my mother too."

"Fat chance of that. You're going to have to get out from under. We'll work something out," he said, but Dallas thought his voice sounded less certain than his words.

Later, when they left the movie house, Dallas thought, If anyone ever asks me about this picture, I won't be able to tell them a thing. She only hoped that Victor wasn't going to discuss it. Her mind had been elsewhere, wondering what she was going to find when she got home.

The house was in total darkness when they arrived. It was only around ten o'clock, but even if her mother was asleep, Dallas thought, she would have left a light on. She started to run up the walk to the front door. "Let me go in first," Victor called out and went ahead of her.

They both pushed through the door at almost the same moment. They could hear her mother's voice in the living room, crooning a ballad in a plaintive voice and strumming softly on her guitar. Dallas threw open the door and switched on the lights.

"Oh, don't do that." Her mother shielded her eyes. "Turn them off." Dallas turned off the overhead light and turned on a shaded lamp instead. In the few seconds of bright light she had seen that her mother's face was streaked with mascara and tears. She looked awful. Andy was stretched out on the floor, on his stomach, sound asleep.

"Are you all right?" Dallas asked.

"I don't know," her mother said in a dull voice. "You have beautiful pink cheeks, Dallas. You look pretty. It must be cold out."

Victor nudged his brother with his foot. "Hey, get up." Victor looked both amused and exasperated by his older brother. Dallas knew that he often felt that his brother got away with murder, and she had sensed earlier in the evening when he had talked about Andy, that Victor had been quite pleased that their father was getting tougher with him. Now he poked at Andy harder. "Get up."

"Lay off," Andy mumbled. Then he sat up and looked at them with sleepy eyes. "What's going on?"

"You tell us," Victor said.

Andy didn't answer, but he stood up. "Where the devil have you been?" he asked Dallas.

"We went to the movies."

"You've been gone a helluva long time. Your mother was afraid to stay alone."

"You didn't have to stay," Mrs. Davis said apologetically. "You could have gone."

"Yeah, and left you here bawling your eyes out." Andy sounded disgusted. "All right, Vic. You want to go."

Victor looked at Dallas. "Go on," she said. "We'll be okay."

After the boys had left, Mrs. Davis looked at her daughter meekly. "I'm sorry, Dallas. I've made an awful fool of myself today, I'm afraid."

"I guess you couldn't help what you did. Come on up to bed now. Do you want some hot milk?"

"That would be very nice." Her mother kept looking at her, as if she wanted something. Love? Approval? Forgiveness? Dallas didn't know what. She herself was so tired from the strain of the day that she was aching to get right into bed. But she took her mother upstairs, and then went down to the kitchen to fix the hot milk. While she was watching the pot so the milk wouldn't boil over, she wondered again if this was going to be her way of life. Was she going to spend it taking care of her mother? She would never get married if her mother was going to have to live with her. Would there ever be any way out?

Dallas watched her mother sit up in bed

and sip the milk like a docile child, and she thought, My father must have loved her a great deal to have taken care of her so much. She had known that he had been the strong one, but she had never realized how much he must have done. But she did not want to be the one to carry on where he had left off. When her mother was finished, Dallas took the empty mug away and kissed her mother good-night.

Her mother squeezed her hand and said, "You're a very good daughter."

Dallas said nothing, but inside she cried, "No, I'm not. I'm not. You don't know, you just don't know how hard it is. You don't know how much I sometimes hate you."

8

"I wish I were dead." Ellen Davis wrote the words in her large, scrawling hand across the page. She sat and stared at the paper for several minutes before she crumped it up and dropped it in the wastebasket.

The whole Thanksgiving weekend had come and gone, but she was still feeling the effects of it. The fact that Christmas was looming ahead did not help. She had said to Dallas that morning, "Let's ignore Christmas. Let's just pretend it doesn't exist. I'd like to go to bed and wake up when it's over. I don't think I can bear it."

But Dallas wouldn't agree. She had said that she wanted a tree. It didn't have to be a big one like those they used to have, but she wanted a tree and presents, and she wanted to invite friends in for Christmas Eve the way they always had. They had gotten into rather an argument about it, the way they did so often lately about everything. "I can't stand it," Ellen said aloud, although there was no one there to hear. She had told Dallas that she was being childish, she was too old for Christmas, and Dallas had accused her of being a child. "You can't crawl into bed and pull the covers over your head," Dallas had shouted at her at one point. "You have to face life. Maybe if you thought of someone else beside yourself for a change. . . ."

That had hurt. Dallas didn't understand; no one understood. Yes, Dallas had lost her father, but that was different, even though their relationship had been close. No one knew how much that closeness had hurt her as Dallas grew older — the way Hank and Dallas had gone off on their jaunts together, had their secrets, as if she didn't count, wasn't part of the family. Ellen had always known that Dallas loved her father more than she did her, and Ellen was still paying for it now. Dallas must wish that she was the one who had died.

So. She was feeling sorry for herself. What was wrong with that? Didn't she have a right?

Ellen got up from the kitchen table and walked around the house restlessly: from the kitchen to the living room, to the dining room, to the sun porch, and back to the kitchen.

The kitchen needed to be painted. The

living-room sofa could use a new slipcover. But she didn't have the energy for any such projects. What was the use of fixing up the house without Hank? Ellen felt a pang of guilt. There was Dallas. The house should be kept up for Dallas, for Dallas and her friends. They came to the house. She shouldn't let it get shabby. If her mother were here, she would scold her, would say that she was lazy, that she was behaving badly. She probably was, but it wasn't laziness. It was the awful feeling that nothing mattered, that nothing made any difference anymore. Thinking that way was not fair to Dallas; Dallas mattered. There her mother would have some reason to criticize her. She wasn't doing a good job with Dallas. She was trying every way; she wanted desperately to be close to Dallas, to be her friend as well as her mother, but Dallas kept pushing her away, and she was vulnerable. An angry word or look from Dallas sent her into a panic, made her feel lost. She felt like someone going backwards; for every forward step she thought she made, she was pushed two steps back.

She poured herself another cup of coffee, glancing at the clock on the kitchen wall. It was beginning to get dark already, and Dallas should be home. She had gone to the library and to do some Christmas shopping with her friend Jennifer. Ellen could feel her awful loneliness, with its ensuing sense of panic, start to creep in as the darkness enveloped the house. She could turn on the lights, but she chose not to. Not yet. It was as if plumbing the depth of her loneliness was some kind of comfort; she had first to go to the limits of her pain in order to find any relief anywhere.

She didn't have to turn on the light. Dallas came in with an armful of bundles, dumped them on the table, and turned the switch. "Why are you standing here in the dark?"

"I don't know. I guess I felt like it. What did you buy?"

"Not to be opened till Christmas."

"Do you need any money?"

"No, I saved out of my allowance. Thank you anyway."

Slowly Ellen felt herself relax. Strangely, she thought, although the tensions between Dallas and herself were irritating, she felt much better when Dallas was home. Tension, she supposed, was better than emptiness.

Dallas hurriedly took her packages out of the room, probably to hide them in her closet. But she soon was downstairs again. "What's for supper?"

"Nothing exciting. I was going to make some hamburgers and salad. Do you want potatoes?"

"I'll fix them if you want me to," Dallas offered.

Ellen could tell that Dallas had something

on her mind, and she was right. As soon as they sat down to eat, Dallas started to speak. "Mom, I want to talk to you about something, and please don't get excited or upset until you hear me out, and really think about it. It's important to me."

"All right. Go ahead." Ellen kept her voice calm, but she had a foreboding of something definitely unpleasant.

"Okay. I'll give it to you straight. Jen said that a bunch of the kids are planning to go up to Vermont the day after Christmas to go skiing. And I want to go with them."

Ellen breathed a sigh of relief. "Well, that's not so terrible. Who all is going?"

"Victor, Jen, and I think Nancy and Sue and a couple of the boys. Andy may come too, I don't know."

"No chaperone?"

"Mom, we don't need a chaperone."

"I think you do. I wouldn't mind —"

Dallas didn't let her finish the sentence. "Now, Mom, please don't misunderstand. This is a kids' party. I don't think anyone wants someone's mother around."

Of course. She should have known. She was always falling into these traps, leaving herself wide open for rejection, when any rejection these days was a deep wound, opening up all the pain of her aloneness. "I didn't think of myself as just someone's mother. I thought

108

your friends liked me, accepted me as a person without hanging a label on me."

"But you're still a mother. Of course they like you, except that. . . ."

"Except what?" Oh, God, why couldn't she shut up and say she didn't care. But she did care. She didn't have the strength to put up a front the way some women did and pretend that life alone, without her Hank, was okay. She couldn't pretend, and she didn't see any sense in doing so anyway. "Have they said anything?"

"Well, no. . . ." Dallas was squirming, and all Ellen's senses were crying out, drop it, drop it, but she couldn't. She had to poke at her own wound.

"Tell me. Have your friends said that they don't like to have me around?" She was looking straight at Dallas, waiting for her answer.

"Not in so many words. They like you, I'm sure they do. But they wouldn't like anyone's mother around all the time, no matter how great she was."

"Maybe you're the one who doesn't want me around," Ellen said, knowing she was opening herself to another hurt.

Dallas gave her a swift glance and then looked away. "That's beside the point. I'm your daughter —"

"And you have to put up with it."

"Mom, let's not go into that. I stayed home

because I thought you needed me, and I wanted to help. But going away for a few days is different."

"But I can't let you go away for a few days with a bunch of kids, because I don't think it's right. I feel a double responsibility. When a girl your age is without a father, it *is* different. I have no one to discuss the plans with, so I do have to be stricter. For my sake as well as yours. This is our loss, Dallas. I don't have a husband and you don't have a father, so we are not like all the other families. You are not like all the other kids."

"It doesn't seem fair." Dallas looked so woebegone that Ellen wished that she could say yes. But she felt that she was right. And also she thought of the long days and nights alone in the house without Dallas, and she knew that her own fears were part of her thinking. She didn't like herself for those secret thoughts, but she felt justified in indulging her own need. Sometime, in some hazy future, she would be able to face being alone, but not yet, not yet.

"I won't spoil your fun," Ellen said, trying to smile. "I'll make myself inconspicuous."

"Maybe I'll stay home," Dallas said glumly.

"That's not fair. That would really make me feel terrible. It will be good for you to go, even with me along. I'm serious about insisting on a chaperone anyway."

"Nuts! You just don't want to stay home alone. Why can't you be honest about it?"

"That's not fair. I do think there should be a chaperone, but what if I don't want to stay home alone? Going off to Vermont would be a nice change for me. Is that a crime?"

"You'll never understand!" Dallas cried, and she got up from the table and went upstairs to her room.

Ellen pushed her own unfinished meal away from her and sat at the table drinking her coffee. She could feel her heart pounding and wondered if she was having a heart attack.

The pounding subsided after a few minutes, but there was no relief from her sense of abandonment.

Ever since Hank had died, her life had been a series of rejections, one after another. She didn't feel as if she belonged anywhere. She loved her house, the rooms that she and Hank had filled over the years, but even here among her own things she felt alone and couldn't sit still for long. She was not a stupid woman, and she knew that she should not cling to Dallas as she was doing, but she also knew that intelligence had little to do with the state of her emotions. Her loss cut through all else, like a bulldozer doggedly making its way through a forest with no thought for any tender shoots in its path. She could not think of herself as a hard or selfish woman, only that she had been so hurt that even as she wished to die, she was fighting for survival at any cost.

It was still very early, just after seven, and Ellen felt that she could not bear another evening in the house. Ellen was sure that she could feel Dallas's resentment creeping down the stairs, pervading the house. Vi often said to stop by whenever she wanted. "If you don't feel like being alone, just come right over," Vi had said many times. Ellen had not done so, but now she put on her coat, called up to Dallas that she was going over to Vi's for a while, and without stopping to phone first went out.

The Waters' house was only a few blocks away, and since it was a bright, moonlit night, Ellen decided to walk rather than get out the car. She enjoyed the walk although she was thinking that she had never walked alone in the dark before.

The house was lit up, but Ellen quickly noticed that the garage doors were open, and one car was gone, the one Vi and Bob used. The other one was there. Her heart gave a little jump of excitement that made her wonder for a minute whether she should turn around and go home. I'm being ridiculous, she told herself. These boys are the sons of my best friend, and besides maybe they have the big car and Vi and Bob are home. Dismissing her wave of excitement as nonsense, she rang the bell.

Andy answered the door. He had on jeans, an old sweat shirt, and was in bare feet. His curly hair was tousled, and he looked utterly surprised to see Ellen. They stared at each other for a second or two. "Come on in," Andy said.

"I just thought I'd drop in for a few minutes to see your folks." Ellen spoke hurriedly to cover her unease. "Are they home?"

Andy shook his head. "No one's home but me. They went to an early movie and then out for dinner. Vic's working tonight."

"Then I guess I should go."

Andy didn't say anything, but she still stood there facing him. She had not seen Andy since Thanksgiving when he had taken her home, and she wanted an opportunity to talk to him. "But maybe I'll warm up for a few minutes first," Ellen said, giving Andy a smile. "That is, if you don't mind."

"I don't mind."

She followed him into the living room and took off her coat. The hi-fi was playing a jazz record. "That music sounds familiar."

"It's an old Dizzy Gillespie record."

There was no use trying to make conversation with Andy. She had already discovered that was a lost cause. Better to say what she had on her mind and then leave. "I guess I owe you an apology for Thanksgiving. My recollection is that I made a fool of myself."

Andy smiled. "You were very seductive."

Ellen blushed. "I was still drunk. And I really was afraid to stay alone. Was I pretty awful?"

"I would not use that word," Andy drawled. "You were kind of funny. I could have taken advantage of you."

Ellen felt her face flaming, but she tried to be dignified. "I don't think so. I wasn't that drunk."

Andy laughed. "You mean you knew what you were doing?"

"No," Ellen said indignantly. "Don't try to trip me up. I mean I would have come to my senses."

"Possibly." Andy still had that smile on his face. "Want to hear another record? How about some Benny Goodman?"

Ellen looked at him defiantly. "You don't have to put on an old record for me."

"I'm not doing it for you. I've been listening to old records all evening. Can I get you a drink?"

"No, thank you."

They sat in silence listening to the music. Andy got a beer for himself and persuaded Ellen to take a glass of wine. Slowly she found herself relaxing, sipping her wine and losing herself in the music, her foot tapping in rhythm to the sound.

"Would you like to dance?"

Ellen was startled by the suggestion. She had been thinking that Andy was being polite and probably feeling sorry for her, which was why he had asked her to stay. She loved dancing, but Hank had not. Although he had liked music and had a good sense of rhythm, he had never danced, and she had missed it. "I don't know if I remember how," she said.

"There's nothing like finding out."

Andy was a beautiful dancer, and after a little bit of uncertainty, while Ellen was getting used to his steps, she was delighted to find how easily she could follow him. She felt as if the clock had been turned back and she was in her teens again dancing with a college boy. For a few golden minutes she could forget her pain, forget the bleakness of her life, and simply lose herself in the physical exuberance of the dance.

"That was wonderful," she said, when the music stopped. "You're a dear to dance with an old lady like me."

"You don't dance like an old lady," Andy said. "Let's try another."

"I think I should go," she said primly. Her mind was hazy about that Thanksgiving night. She remembered feeling dizzy and clinging to Andy, asking him not to leave her alone. She did not want again to be accused of being seductive. Not by this handsome young man — boy — a boy who looked and acted older than his years and who had a provocative self-contained air that put her on the defensive, but also reminded her that she used to be considered a very attractive woman. She was uneasy with Andy; whether because of her own emotional state or because she suspected he could be blunt at times, she wasn't sure.

He did not give her a chance to think. He put on another record, and they danced again.

They were still dancing when the door opened and Vi and Bob Waters came in. Vi showed her surprise at finding Ellen there, but she quickly covered it and said warmly, "How nice to find you here. I'm glad Andy was home."

"I felt lonesome and I just stopped by. Andy kept me here dancing." Ellen was embarrassed. Both Vi and Bob were pretending that it was quite natural to find Ellen in their house dancing with their son, but she could feel the strain. "I really have to go now."

Bob Waters gave her a sidelong glance and tried to make a joke. "I hope we haven't interrupted anything."

"Oh, Bob, don't be silly," his wife said.

"I'll walk you home," Andy offered.

"No, thank you. I'll be all right." Ellen wanted to leave and leave in a hurry. She did not want Andy to walk her home, and while he looked all innocence, she had a feeling that he was deliberately trying to give his parents the wrong impression.

"No, it's late. I'll take you."

Ellen said good-bye hurriedly and went out.

Furious with Andy, she walked quickly and in silence.

"What's the matter?" Andy asked.

"I really didn't need anyone to walk me home."

Andy took her arm. "Is there anything wrong with my taking you home? It's late and it's dark."

"No, there isn't anything wrong."

When they got to her door, Ellen turned around to say good-night. "Aren't you going to ask me in?" Andy asked. His hand was still on her arm.

"No, Andy, I'm not," she said, but there he was, with that mischievous grin on his face and the moonlight giving a glow to his dark hair. They stood there looking at each other, and Ellen wondered if he could hear her heart hammering. How she missed just the simple touch of a man's hand, of an arm. For weeks after Hank had died she walked with her fist tight in her pocket because she had longed so for his hand in hers, the way they had so often walked together. Her whole body was aching to let Andy put his arms around her, to let her longing take over. . . .

"I'm not such a kid," Andy said. "I've got feelings too, you know."

"Of course I know." Ellen moved away from him and risked a laugh. "I've got to go in. I enjoyed dancing with you, and you were nice to suggest it."

"If that's the way you want it," Andy said, but he was still looking at her knowingly, as if he realized exactly what was going through her mind.

"I guess it is," she mumbled, confused, and went into the house. She felt stirred up and wondered what she would have done if Andy had persisted. But Andy wouldn't do that. He would never coax, and she knew that if there were to be any move it would be up to her. The whole idea was repugnant and frightening and tantalizing: another phase of being a widow. She was not even thinking of sex. That was something she did not want to consider at all. Just dealing with her need for some physical contact with a man was enough to try to sort out for now. But the answer couldn't be Andy. She'd have to be sick to think of Andy in any other role than as the son of her good friends. She was like a beggar, picking up tiny crumbs of affection anywhere she could.

Wearily she went upstairs to bed, grateful that Dallas's light was out. She wasn't up to facing Dallas now. How awful, Ellen thought, that for a few moments of pleasure she had to pay such a high price emotionally. It was as if she were an adolescent again, trying to find her place, trying to learn where she belonged, and to whom. She felt like a wandering soul. And all she could see ahead was more desolation.

9

The first snow fell a few days before Christmas. Dallas jumped out of bed when she saw the white flakes dashing against her window and ran to look out. She always felt excited by the beauty of the first snowfall. Nothing looked ordinary anymore. The commonplace houses, the familiar street became transformed, like a girl dressed up for a party. Dallas opened her window, gathered up a handful of the lovely white stuff, and washed her face in it.

"Mom, it's snowing." Dallas put on a robe and ran down the stairs to the kitchen where her mother was already having her morning coffee.

"I can see it," her mother said drily.

"Isn't it beautiful!"

"I'm thinking about who's going to shovel it."

Dallas's face fell. Of course. Her father was the one who previously would have been out

119

there with a shovel, clearing a path to the garage, clearing the walk from the house. But Christmas was only a few days away, the first snow was coming down, and Dallas was not going to let her mother dampen her spirits. "I'll shovel it. I can do it."

"I should help you," her mother said half-heartedly.

"You don't have to. I'll be okay."

"What would I do without you?" Her mother's arms were around her in a tight hug, until Dallas wriggled herself free. "You're a beautiful girl."

"I'm not," Dallas murmured, uncomfortable under her mother's wistful affection.

They sat down to breakfast, and Dallas's mother broke a slice of toast into small pieces, as if eating were too much of an effort. She said, "I'd like to go to bed and wake up when Christmas is over."

"Do you want to get the tree today?" Dallas asked, determinedly cheerful.

"All right if you insist. I could do without it."

"You said we could have one."

"I guess I hoped you would change your mind," her mother said heavily.

"I haven't."

After breakfast Dallas put on warm slacks and a heavy sweater, and she got the snow shovel out of the garage. She felt good in the brisk air, and she quite liked the idea that she was carrying out a job that had been her father's. The doing of it made her feel close to him without the depression that had come to accompany her thoughts of him. And it was satisfying to see a smooth path slowly emerge, with the snow neatly piled on each side. But the work was tiring. Soon her arms began to ache, and the walk to the house seemed much longer than she thought it to be. She should have cleared the driveway first.

"Hello." Dallas turned, and there was Victor, pink cheeked, his red woolen cap bright against the snow. With a snow shovel in his hand, he was a welcome sight indeed. "I thought you might need some help."

Dallas threw her arms around him. "You *are* an angel. If you want to do the driveway, I'll finish the walk."

"Okay." But first he leaned his shovel against the house and tackled her in the snow.

"Angel my eye, you devil. . . ." They were both rolling in the snow, laughing, getting wet, until finally Dallas shook herself free and put a handful of snow down Victor's neck.

"Oh, boy, I'll get you for that!" He had her down again, burying her face in the snow until she cried for help.

They were laughing and floundering in the snow when her mother came to the door. Her face was stained with tears. "Oh, Dallas, Dallas. . . ."

Dallas jumped up and shook the snow from

121

her clothes. "What's the matter? What happened?" She ran up to the door, and Victor followed.

"Nothing happened, but I feel terrible. I'm so ashamed. Today's our wedding anniversary, and to think I almost forgot. I've lost track of dates, and I just happened to look at the calendar. We would have been married nineteen years today."

Dallas put her arms around her mother and went inside with her. "Don't feel so bad. It's good that you almost forgot. I mean —"

Her mother pulled away from her. "It's not good. It's awful. I can't forget. I'm not built that way."

"I don't want you to forget him. I never will either," Dallas said. "I just think you shouldn't make a big thing out of dates. You shouldn't add to your mourning with dates."

"How can I not?" Her mother heaved a long sigh. "Everyone says time will help, but it just seems to make things worse."

"You're not giving yourself a chance. Come on and get dressed, and we'll go for the tree. It's so beautiful out."

"It's too beautiful." Her mother turned to Victor. "Forgive me for making a scene. I can't help it."

"Don't mind me. I'll go with you for the tree if you want. I'm good at picking one out."

"That will be nice." Mrs. Davis gave him a weak smile.

Her mother went upstairs to get dressed, and when she came down she was brighter. The thought struck Dallas that her mother could brighten up for about everyone except her daughter. While she was grateful that Victor was there, she resented the fact that she seemed to be the main recipient of her mother's grieving. Maybe her mother's behavior was only natural, but the burden was too much.

Although Mrs. Davis had said she didn't want a Christmas tree, she was fussy about buying one. It had to be exactly the right shape and the right height. Finally they picked one out, and Victor put it in the trunk of the car and tied the lid down over it.

They brought it home and set it up in the living room. Dallas immediately brought out the lights and ornaments that had been boxed away the year before. Victor stayed to help, and he and Dallas decorated the tree. In the afternoon Jennifer and Nancy and some of the boys came over, and they made a fire in the fireplace and popped corn. Dallas was glad to see that her mother's gloom had disappeared and she seemed to be having a good time.

Before Victor left he took Dallas aside to talk about the ski trip. "You shouldn't stay home because of your mother," he said. "I won't go if you don't, and I want to go."

"I don't want you to stay home because of me." Dallas felt caught in a dilemma. "I'm afraid she may spoil the trip for everybody."

"She won't. Don't worry. Maybe Andy will be her date," Victor said mischievously.

Dallas made a grimace. "Is he definitely coming?"

"He says so. All his friends are at college. I guess he's pretty bored at home, and he's mad for skiing. Anyway we're going, you and me and your ma. That's definite."

"Whatever you say, Mr. Macho." Dallas made a deep bow and then kissed him on the nose.

When everyone had gone, Dallas said, "It really feels like Christmas, doesn't it?"

"It did for a little while," her mother said.

"Let's have our supper by the fire. It will be cozy," Dallas suggested.

"That sounds pleasant," her mother agreed, visibly trying to stay cheerful. "I'll fix something special. Would you like a quiche?"

"Super." Dallas set a small table for them in front of the fire, but by the time they sat down to eat she saw that her mother had to make a conscious effort to keep up her spirits. More than once she caught her mother staring moodily into the fire, and she knew where her thoughts were. She seemed genuinely pleased, though, when Dallas told her she had decided to go on the ski trip and that Ellen could come along.

How can you sympathize with someone, love her, and yet sometimes not love her at all? Dallas sat in front of the tree on Christmas morning, feeling as full of despair as her mother looked. Her heart went out to her, and yet she kept thinking, Sometimes I don't love my mother. . . . Time is supposed to help, but how long will it take? When will she let me go? When will she let us both start living again? She wanted to help her, but there was nothing more that she could do. A short while before Christmas, Dallas had suggested timidly that perhaps her mother could go to see a psychologist or psychiatrist. But her mother had rejected that idea quickly. "What can a psychiatrist do? No one can bring Hank back to life for me. There's nothing the matter with me; the problem is what life has done."

Dallas could tell by her mother's face that there was no use arguing the point. She had wanted to say that perhaps her mother could be helped in her attitude, but she didn't dare.

Their friends had been generous, and there were plenty of presents to open, but after everything was admired, clothes tried on, and the torn paper thrown into the fireplace, the day dragged. Mrs. Davis had refused to accept any of the invitations they'd received for Christmas dinner. "Thanksgiving was enough," she said. "I couldn't bear being the fifth wheel at a family Christmas dinner." Then she added, "But you can go out if you want to." Dallas knew that was a ridiculous offer. Her mother would have a fit if she said yes, and she wouldn't dream of leaving her.

Dallas could see, however, that her mother was making a real effort to give her a good Christmas. Instead of the usual Christmas dinner, her mother fixed a special shrimp dish that was Dallas's favorite. She also opened a bottle of wine, and in a poignant way she tried to make the meal festive without being pointedly Christmasy. When they sat down to eat, her mother talked about some of the Christmas dinners she had eaten alone with her mother when she was a child and her father was on the road. "They were awful Christmases," her mother said. "My mother would be furious that he didn't get home and took out her feelings on me. My father always sent me fabulous presents, huge dolls and once there was a beautiful dollhouse. I think my mother was jealous. I think I vowed even then," her mother said with a wistful smile, "that if I ever had a daughter she would be my friend. You are my friend, aren't you, Dallas?"

Dallas thought a minute before she answered. "I am your friend, but I think I'm your daughter first. It's different."

A hurt look crossed her mother's face, but she covered it quickly. "I suppose it is," she said lightly. Dallas wished she knew how to tell her that she wanted a mother, not a girl friend, and wondered if a too loving mother could be as bad as an unloving one.

She was relieved when after dinner her mother suggested a movie and was glad that when they came home it was ten o'clock and a reasonable time to go to bed. The next day they would be going away skiing. Dallas was happy that she had decided to go, even though her mother was coming along.

The next day was a perfect winter's day. The snow was still on the ground and had a hard crust on it; the air was dry and brisk. Dallas was taking their car and picking up first Andy and Victor and then Jen on the way. The others were going in another car.

At the Waters' house, Andy greeted her mother with a sardonic grin. "Do you ski as well as you dance?" he asked. Dallas was surprised to see her mother blush.

"No, I don't," Mrs. Davis said vehemently.

"You sure you want to go with these kids?" Vi asked.

"I'll be their chaperone," Mrs. Davis said.

"Some chaperone. We'll have to watch you so you don't get loaded," Andy remarked, still grinning. Her mother gave him a dirty look.

"Andy!" Vi remonstrated. "Don't pay any attention to him," she said to Ellen. "He's a terrible tease."

"I think I can take care of myself," Ellen said with some dignity.

They met the other car, with Nancy Edwards, Sue Prince, Ted Bateman, and Joel Kirkman in it, and they followed it to the highway. It was a four-hour drive up to the ski area in Vermont. Dallas and Jen had agreed before that they wanted to room together, but when they got to the motel, Mrs. Davis objected. Nancy and Sue were taking one room, which left her in a room alone.

"That's what I assumed you would want," Dallas said to her mother.

"I don't like to be in this big double room by myself, and there's no such thing as a single, which I wouldn't want anyway. If they put up a cot, the three girls can share one room and you can come in with me. It'll be cheaper that way anyway."

"We're not worried about the money," Jen said mildly.

"You women make up your minds," Andy said. "We're going to dump our stuff and get out on the slope." The four boys went off to their double rooms.

128

"We just need two rooms," Mrs. Davis said to the man at the desk, "and you can put a cot in one of them."

The girls looked at each other as Mrs. Davis took the keys and got directions to find their rooms. "It doesn't matter," Nancy whispered to Dallas. "We're only going to sleep in the rooms anyway."

But Dallas was furious. Once in the room with her mother, she said, "I don't think you should be the one to tell everyone where to sleep. Jen and I wanted to be together."

Her mother didn't look up from the bag she was unpacking. "The girls didn't seem to mind." Then she swung around and faced Dallas. "You're the one who's bothered. You're critical of everything I do. You're worse than my mother! Let's try to have a good time these few days, Dallas."

"I want to. But I didn't expect to share a room with my mother."

Her mother looked at her with hurt eyes. "You make me sound like a monster. Is it so terrible to be with your mother?"

"Oh, Mom, we've gone over this before. You're a great person, but think of your mother. You don't want her to come to visit you. Why don't you want her around?"

"Because she always puts me down," Ellen said. "I try so hard with you, but nothing I seem to do is right."

"Maybe you're trying too hard."

"See, there you go again. I try too hard, or I don't try enough. Why can't you be as nice to me as you are to Jennifer, to your friends? What's so awful about wanting to share a room with my own daughter? If my mother had ever treated me like a friend, like someone she loved and admired, I would have been deliriously happy. We should be close now, Dallas. We need each other."

Her mother's eyes were fastened on her pleadingly. Dallas looked away before she answered. "I wish I knew how to say it right."

"Say it. Tell me, what am I doing wrong?"

Dallas was groping for the right words. "There's a difference between loving and needing. Of course we need each other, but not in the way you think. You need your own life, and I need mine, and they're different."

"But I have no life. You are my only life now. Don't take it away from me. That would be too cruel."

Dallas felt hopeless. She couldn't come out and tell her mother that she was a burden, that what her mother thought was close was pushing Dallas farther and farther from her. She didn't say anything, but went on with her unpacking.

Out on the slope Dallas forgot her troubles. She loved to ski, and gliding down the crusty snow she felt marvelous, like a bird flying. Her mother was on the beginner's slope, and after several runs, Dallas felt obligated to go over to see how she was doing.

"I'm having a terrible time," Mrs. Davis said crossly. "I'm glad you came over. Maybe you can help me. I'm falling all over the place."

Good-naturedly, Dallas stayed with her mother and tried to teach her how to manage her skis. "Dad would have loved being here. He was a beautiful skier," Dallas remarked.

Her mother gave her a sharp look. "You mean you wouldn't have had to help him."

"You misunderstand everything I say." Oh Lord, Dallas thought, I have to watch every word. How nice getting away from her for a few days would have been. But, damn it, I'm not going to let her spoil my skiing.

They stayed out until it got dark and then gathered at the Ski Shack to warm up by the fire. That evening everyone was tired and went to bed early.

The next day Dallas and her friends stayed out on the slopes the whole morning. Dallas spent some time with her mother, but Mrs. Davis gave up and said she'd go into the Shack and read. Dallas and Victor decided to try cross-country skiing in the afternoon.

"Do you know your way around up here?"

Mrs. Davis asked at lunch, when Dallas mentioned their plan. "Won't you get lost?"

"No, of course not. Don't worry about us. We'll be fine."

"Maybe you'd like to spend the afternoon in a bar with me," Andy said to Mrs. Davis. "That'll take your mind off Dallas."

"And what is that remark supposed to mean?" Mrs. Davis's eyes flashed at Andy, but he kept looking at her innocently.

"It means it would be good for you to forget about Dallas once in a while. Have some fun on your own." Andy spoke as if he meant what he said, and Mrs. Davis was obviously taken aback.

"I don't think I need your advice about what I should do," Mrs. Davis said coldly.

"Can't blame me for trying," Andy said good-naturedly. "Just thought someone ought to tell you you're too wrapped up in your daughter, and there's a big world out there to enjoy."

"He's got a point," Dallas murmured.

Her mother turned to her. "I'm glad everyone's so concerned about me." She was furious. Dallas thought that Andy's remark had hit home, and she was glad he had said what he did.

After lunch Dallas and Victor rented the skis they needed for going cross-country. When Dallas told her mother that she and

Victor were leaving, she said, "Why don't you go and have a drink with Andy later? It might be fun."

Her mother surprised her by saying, "Sometimes I think you kids are making fun of me. At times you make me feel so good, and at other times when I'm with all of you I feel a million years old. No, I don't want to have a drink with Andy. I'll stay in and read."

Dallas didn't know whether she was feeling sorry for herself or if she preferred to be alone. She bent down and gave her a kiss before she left.

10

There wasn't much chance for talking as Dallas and Victor skied across the open fields. The snow-covered countryside glistened under a brilliant sun. They went through some patches of woods, and when they came out into the sunshine again, Dallas was so warm she stripped off her top sweater and tied it around her waist.

They must have gone miles, Dallas thought, when Victor suggested they sit down on some rocks and rest. They both took off their skis and turned their faces up to the sun.

"This is heavenly," Dallas murmured. "The best I've felt for months."

"I've been worrying about you. You've been

awfully distant." Victor was examining her face.

"I suppose I have." She sat up from her reclining position. "I wish I could talk about my father. Everything seems to be bottled up inside of me. I can't talk about him at home. My mother keeps misunderstanding. It sounds crazy, but I don't feel as if it's right for me — well, to love anyone, to be involved so soon after he died."

"That's crazy," Victor agreed.

"It's as if I have to get my feelings straightened out first."

"You need to get straightened out with your mother."

"Don't I know it! But how do you go about doing that?"

"By doing something absolutely independent, taking some step on your own. You've got to break away."

"You mean go away?"

"That could be one way. But even while you're home, you've got to have something private, something that's yours alone."

"Easier said than done. I'll think about it."

"Thinking's not going to help." Suddenly Victor's arms were around her, and he was kissing her and holding her tenderly. Dallas felt a great surge of warmth for him, and with the sun on her face she responded to him happily.

When they pulled apart, Victor was gazing at her seriously. "You remember what I said to you about going to school in the fall. I'm going to do it. And if you went to school too, and we both worked, we could get married. Nothing would hurt you then. I would be your protection. . . ."

Dallas looked at him in wonder. "You make everything sound so simple. I couldn't get married. I'm not eighteen yet."

"I don't mean we have to set a date now, but let's plan to get married. I love you, Dallas."

"I love you too." Her arms were around him, and she was clinging to him. She could feel the strength of his body against hers, and she thought, This is ours, ours alone. No one can touch it; no one can spoil this. Standing close, with their arms around each other, in the wide expanse of the snow-covered fields, Dallas knew that she would remember this time always: the snow and the sun, and Victor's cold cheeks against hers.

When she finally pulled away from him, she stretched out her arms. "We'll talk about it. We have lots of time."

"I'm very serious," Victor said.

They put on their skis and turned back to the beginning of the trail. Dallas felt lighthearted and happy.

* * *

"You see, we came back in one piece," Dallas said to her mother gaily.

"I'm glad of that." They were in their room, and Dallas was about to take a shower and get dressed for the evening. She felt elated. Maybe Victor was right. Even the knowledge of their private conversation gave her the feeling of a protective wall, a comforting defense against her own irritability with her mother. How wonderful if all the little annoyances of living with her mother did not bother her because she had her own secret life! Sometimes I don't love my mother, I think. . . . But if she let herself love someone else, if she was secretly engaged to Victor, perhaps her feelings for her mother would not be so erratic. They wouldn't matter so much.

Spontaneously she gave her mother a hug. "You see, you mustn't worry about me so much."

"I worried all afternoon. Are you wearing slacks tonight or your long skirt?"

"I'll wear my denim skirt. I think there's a discotheque down the road where we're going dancing."

"Then I'll put on a long skirt too."

Of course her mother would be coming along, but she didn't care. She wasn't going to argue or fight anymore.

*　*　*

137

When they arrived at the discotheque, the place was jammed with teen-agers. "Oh, it's so crowded," Mrs. Davis said. "Do we have to stay here?"

"I'll run you back to the motel if you'd rather," Andy offered, but Ellen shook her head. "If all of you want to stay, I will too."

The group managed to squeeze in at two small tables off in a corner, and as soon as the music started, everyone got up to dance. That left Mrs. Davis sitting alone, trying, not too successfully, to look at ease. The floor was crowded, but Dallas and Victor danced well together, and she was having a good time. But before the music stopped, Dallas said, "We'd better go back and sit with my mother a bit."

"You are a darling," Mrs. Davis said to Victor, as if returning to sit with her had been Victor's idea.

"I love dancing," Mrs. Davis remarked.

"Do you want to try the next one with me?" Victor asked.

"I'd be delighted," Mrs. Davis said brightly.

When the others came back to the table, Andy sat down next to Mrs. Davis, and Dallas heard him order a drink for her. "Drink it slowly," he said in his teasing voice, "and it won't hit you. It's all in knowing how."

He was not letting up on her mother, but Dallas was rather pleased to see that her mother, rather than being annoyed, was getting back at him. "You're obviously very experienced," her mother said, sipping her drink, "but I think I'll give *you* a little advice for a change."

"And what's that?" Andy said.

"How about making up your mind where you fit in? You don't seem to be able to decide whether you're a kid or an adult." She smiled at him smoothly.

"That's some advice coming from you. People in glass houses . . . ."

Her mother flushed. Andy was hitting home again. "I know very well who I am," Mrs. Davis said. "I'm a mother."

"We all know that," Andy said, in a voice that implied he didn't think much of her motherhood.

The music started then, and Victor said to Mrs. Davis, "Let's have our dance."

Dallas shook her head when Andy asked her to dance. "I'll watch this one," she said, and he went off with Jen. Alone at the table, Dallas watched her mother trying her best to follow Victor's steps on the crowded floor. She felt both sorry and embarrassed for her. Her young-looking mother looked old and rather foolish amidst all the teen-agers. Dallas's throat felt choked, and she wasn't sure whether her sadness came from affection or annoyance.

Her thoughts were interrupted by a tall, bearded man who was suddenly standing by her table. He was much older than she, probably older than her mother, and Dallas's first thought was to wonder what was he doing there. When he spoke he had a slight foreign accent. "Would you care to dance?" he asked Dallas. "I saw you here alone, and it seemed a pity for you to sit and for me to sit with such music playing."

He stood tall and straight and was distinguished looking. Dallas thought he might be a professor from the college nearby. She was intrigued and said that she would be delighted. He danced well, although remarking that he could only dance to slow music like the number that had just began. Dallas was amused by the looks her friends gave her when they saw her on the floor with him. He said he was a visiting professor in Russian studies at the college and that he came to the discotheque because he was very interested in what young Americans did. He asked if he might come to see her at her home and was disappointed when she told him that she was only visiting in the area.

Her mother and Victor had stopped and gone back to their table. Across the floor Dallas caught her mother staring at her with a worried frown on her face. When the music stopped, her escort led her back to her table, bowed from the waist, and thanked her for the dance.

"Who was that?" her mother demanded.

"I don't know his name. He's a professor at the college. A visiting professor in Russian studies, and he's interested in American young people."

"You mean that's what he told you," her mother fairly shrieked. "I'll say he's interested, coming here to pick up some young girl. That man is older than your father. Haven't you got more sense than to fall for that? An old man like that comes to a place like this for only one reason — to find some foolish girl like you!"

"You're a fine one to talk!" Dallas was furious. "Andy was right. People in glass houses . . . . What are you doing here with a bunch of kids? You have no business bawling me out. How do you think you look, sitting here with us, dancing with kids, flirting with boys half your age? You'd better not tell me what to do. I don't have to stand it anymore. I'm leaving." Dallas marched toward the door, and Victor quickly followed her.

Jen ran after them. "Don't go. Please stay."

"I can't. I'm sorry. I hope the evening hasn't been spoiled for everyone."

"Don't worry about that," Jen said. "Are you okay?"

"I suppose so," Dallas said morosely.

Victor drove her home in silence. When

they got to the motel, he said, "Come to my room, We can watch some television."

"Okay." She certainly didn't feel like going into the room she shared with her mother.

Victor switched on the TV, and Dallas sat on the bed to watch. But she wasn't seeing anything. Her eyes blurred, and then she burst into tears. Victor's arms were around her. "Cry it out," he said.

She leaned against him, sobbing. "I don't know what to do. There's no end to it. Every time I try to be friends with her, she starts something all over again. . . . I can't stand it anymore. . . ."

"Just relax. Cry. You'll feel better." Victor was holding her close, patting the hair away from her face.

The warmth of his arms was comforting, and soon she stopped her hard sobbing. "She lets all her hurt and angry feelings out on me. I wish I knew what to do."

"Remember what I said this afternoon. You have to make a break." He jumped up and went to the door and locked it.

"Dallas, remember what I said this afternoon? Let's make a real commitment to each other. I love you, and you love me. We need each other. Let's make love, really. You'll — we'll — have something that no one can touch, not even your mother. It will be just yours and mine."

"Do you really think so?" she asked, nervously aware of her own strong desire to forget all else in Victor's arms.

"I know so." Victor stood over her, smiling, and pulled her to her feet. "I love you, Dallas. We love each other, we're going to be married sometime, we belong to each other."

Dallas stood facing him, holding both his hands tightly in each of her own. "I love you, too, Victor," she said seriously. He pulled her to him and kissed her, tenderly first, then harder, and Dallas felt a delicious warmth spread through her. Why not? she thought, and tried to ignore the nagging little question at the back of her mind. Maybe Victor was right; maybe they should just let go and enjoy what they had with each other.

"Dallas, let's get into bed where it's warm," whispered Victor. They turned, and suddenly the bed looked huge to Dallas. It seemed to take up the entire room. All at once she pulled away and sat down on a chair.

"I can't do it. I can't," she whispered.

Victor knelt in front of her. "Don't be scared. If we love each other, it's all right. We're not strangers, and we're not kids anymore. It's going to be all right. Dallas, I love you so much."

Dallas shook her head. "I can't." She sat silent for a few minutes, running her fingers through Victor's hair. "No. You see, Victor,

143

I'd be doing it for the wrong reason: to get back at my mother. I don't want that. She would be part of this, the way she is everything else in my life. It's no good, Victor. I feel as if she's right in this room with us now. It won't work."

Victor groaned and stood up. He sat down on the bed with his head in his hands. "But I love you, Dallas," he mumbled.

"It has nothing to do with you, don't you see? When we get together, it's got to be just you and me, without my mother mixed up in it. God, I don't want to make *love* because of her. It's too important. You said it's very private, but if I'm doing it because I'm mad at my mother, it's not private anymore. And she'd always be part of it. You've got to understand."

"I suppose I do," Victor said reluctantly. "I suppose you know your own feelings."

"I think I may be beginning to. Let's go out for a walk."

"Okay."

Outside, arm in arm with Victor, the cold night air hit Dallas with a refreshing briskness. She felt that she had accomplished something tremendous that night. She didn't at all know what she was going to do, but she felt that she had acquired a nugget of understanding, of self-awareness that was valuable. She seemed to have stepped out of a fog, and now with luck perhaps she could find the right direction in which to go.

When she got back to her room, she got into bed quickly and pretended to be asleep when her mother came in a short while later. Dallas didn't want anything to touch the good feeling that she had, although she didn't think that her mother would talk about the evening. Her mother had a knack of backing away from arguments and behaving as if they had not happened. She would withdraw into silence until ordinary, daily communication filled in the gap.

II

Dallas still felt confident when she came home. They managed to get through New Year's Eve by paying no attention to it. "It's just another night, Mom. I hate New Year's celebrations." Dallas honestly felt that way, and her only acknowledgment of the occasion was to invite Victor over for dinner and agree to the opening of a bottle of champagne. When her mother wept at midnight, Dallas tried to comfort her. Soon after she sent Victor home and went to bed herself. Her one big New Year's resolution was not to let her mother's tears ruin her life.

She was beginning to see that she had to plan for the future. Until then she felt that she had been marking time and getting lost in the maze of her mother's unhappiness. In the long run her mother was going to have to face her own life; Dallas could not solve her mother's problems for her.

Easier said than done. For all her fine resolutions, Dallas found herself getting caught up again in the daily irritations of her life with her mother. The guitar lessons had petered out over the holidays, and no one seemed to want to start them again. Her mother made no effort to fill her days. In the past few months Dallas had mentioned that she was thinking of going out to look for a job, but her mother had discouraged her. Now she decided that was the first thing she had to do: find a temporary job, since she was still hoping to go away to school in the fall.

Her mother again was not encouraging. "What will I do here all day alone?" Mrs. Davis asked.

"I guess what you do when I'm home. I may not even get a job, but I'm going to try. I'd like to have some money of my own."

"I thought I was very generous with you."

"That's not the point, Mom. You *are* generous, but I want to make some money myself. I need to get out of the house. I'm sick of doing nothing."

"But you're doing a lot, being here with me. Don't you think that's important?"

Dallas faced her mother. "I shouldn't be

with you twenty-four hours a day. You don't want to let me out of your sight. I feel as if I can't breathe anymore. It's not good for you; I know it's not. Can't you see what you've been doing?"

Her mother looked stunned. "I thought you understood." She spoke in a low voice. "I thought you knew you were the only one I had left, that you were my only reason to get out of bed each morning. . . ."

"But I *can't* be," Dallas said vehemently. "You're asking the impossible. You're asking me to exist only for you. Dad had his own life, but you want to own me completely."

Her mother didn't say anything. She just sat staring off into space. Finally she said, "What kind of job are you going to look for?" Her voice sounded tired.

"I don't know. Whatever I can get." Dallas didn't know whether to approach her mother or not. She was afraid that if she made a gesture, her mother would push her away. Their emotions lay between them like a heavy fog in the room until, wordlessly, Dallas went out.

Dallas scanned the newspapers every day, but there were no jobs for someone with no experience. Too many people were out of work.

Then one day she ran into a piece of luck. On one of her frequent trips to the library, the head librarian asked if she knew any young person who might want a part-time job doing clerical work. "We need someone to make out the cards for the new books, catalogue them, and put them in the stacks."

Dallas jumped at the opportunity. "What about me? I think I could do that. I'd love to work here."

"I'd like that fine." The librarian was enthusiastic. "I have to take it up with the library board, and I'll let you know. There's not much pay, and there won't be more than probably twenty hours a week."

"I don't care. It would suit me perfectly."

Dallas went home feeling ecstatic, but she was not surprised that her mother had little to say. Ever since she had expressed herself so strongly, Mrs. Davis had seemed withdrawn. When she got a call about a week later that the job was hers, her mother still didn't react. The next Saturday morning Dallas started to work.

Dallas wondered why she hadn't taken this step before. The hours that she spent working in the library seemed to her the happiest she had had since her father died. It was such a relief to be out of the house, away from her mother, and not to feel guilty, as she would if she were out having a good time someplace. She was working, earning money, and that made a difference. A big difference. As she thought about the last months, however, she came to the conclusion that she hadn't been ready to get out before. She couldn't have left her mother alone any sooner.

Not that she was gone that much. As the librarian had said, she worked only twenty hours a week, five hours on Saturday and five hours three afternoons a week. Yet Dallas soon discovered that her mother would make her pay for this small step toward independence. Dallas didn't know whether her mother was consciously punishing her, but either way her behavior was just as painful.

Little as her mother had done before, she did almost nothing now. She seemed to have completely given up any interest in living. Each afternoon that Dallas came home from work, she found her mother sitting in front of the television set, watching a soap opera, usually with a cup of cold coffee nearby. She didn't do any shopping; she had nothing in the house for their supper.

"You're the wage earner," she said to Dallas with a weak smile. "You can decide what to eat."

Dallas went out as cheerfully as she could to market, and by the time she had their supper ready her mother cheered up some. But the next day was the same all over again.

"I guess I have to learn to be alone," her mother said wearily one evening, "but so far I don't seem to be able to."

"But you were alone during the day when Dad was alive," Dallas pointed out.

"That was different. I knew he was coming home in the evening. I had a reason to market, to cook. I had a reason to live."

"I thought I was your reason to live now," Dallas said. "I'm here. I come home. For heaven's sake, Mom, get with it."

"I'm sorry I'm such a drag," her mother said. But nothing changed.

Sometimes Dallas thought that if her mother drank, if she were an alcoholic, the problem might be easier. There might be a cure for alcoholism; but this listlessness, her total immersion in her own sorrow seemed to have no solution. She refused to see a psychiatrist, insisting that there was nothing wrong with her. She seemed truly to believe that she was behaving naturally for someone recently widowed.

Dallas had been working at the library for a few weeks when Jennifer came in one afternoon all excited. "Have you talked to Victor today?"

Dallas shook her head. "No, he's coming over later."

"He'll tell you about it then. But I met Andy. He's buying a van he wants to take to California, and he wants passengers to help pay expenses. The trip won't cost much, if he gets enough people, except for the fare back.

He wants to stay out West. I want to go. It would be terrific to see Yosemite and the Grand Canyon. You've got to come."

"I'd love nothing better, and I have some Christmas money my grandparents sent me." Then Dallas's face fell. "My mother would never let me go. Don't count on me."

"You've got to go. Forget your mother, Dallas. Andy said Victor wants to come, but he won't without you. By the summer your mother will be okay."

"Not the way she's going now. She's worse, if anything."

"We'll probably only be gone about four weeks. I want to see something of California once we get there. Let's talk about it. Andy wants to get together tonight. I suppose your house as usual?"

"As usual," Dallas said glumly. "I wonder where Andy's getting the money for a van," she mused.

"You know Andy. He has a way of getting what he wants. Maybe he borrowed it. I don't know and I don't care, so long as he has it. It's a fantastic opportunity, Dallas, and you and Victor have to come."

That evening Victor and Andy came over, armed with road maps, tourist's books, and large bags of potato chips and pretzels. Soon Jennifer, Nancy, and her boyfriend Ted joined the group.

Nancy counted noses, "Andy, Victor and Dallas, Jen, Ted and me. Six of us. That's just about right, isn't it, Andy?"

"We could squeeze in one more. I think, but six would be okay."

They were discussing whether to go to New Orleans and across the South through the desert or to keep to the North, when Mrs. Davis appeared. Dallas had purposely not told her about the proposed trip.

"What's going on?" she asked.

Andy explained to her. "Are all of you going?" she asked. "You didn't say a word to me," she said to Dallas.

"It all just came up today. I have the money Grandpa sent me, and we'll only be gone three or four weeks." Dallas spoke quickly. "We're only driving with Andy one way, and then I'd fly back and be home in no time."

"That's not the point. You know how I feel about a chaperone, Dallas. Just you kids alone. . . ." Mrs. Davis looked from one to the other. "And don't tell me about other parents. I don't care what other parents do. I'm in a different position."

"I'm not a kid," Andy stated flatly. "And, if you don't mind my saying so, I think you're being ridiculous."

"I do mind your saying so, very much. I think this is between Dallas and me, and we do not need a public discussion."

"Maybe we do," Victor said. "Don't you

153

trust me? What do you think is going to happen anyway?"

"'The matter has nothing to do with trust. I do not want my daughter, not yet eighteen, traipsing across the country in a van with a bunch of kids. You may not think yourself a kid, Andy, but that's a matter of opinion."

"What do you suggest?" Victor demanded, looking as if he wanted to strangle her.

"I will discuss this with Dallas alone," Mrs. Davis said.

"I know what you're going to suggest. You'll say that you want to come along," Victor said.

"And would that be so terrible?"

Dallas could see that her mother was close to tears by this time, and she had that defenseless, hurt look Dallas had come to know so well. Dallas didn't think she could bear a tearful scene with her mother in front of her friends.

"We'll talk about it later, Vic. We're only in a planning stage now anyway, Mom." Dallas stood up. "I'm going in to make a pot of coffee."

Victor followed her into the kitchen. "You can't let her get away with this, honey. It's too much. She's not going to push herself into this trip."

"I don't want to talk about it now." She put her arms around Victor and leaned her head against his chest. "I can't even think straight anymore."

154

"You're going to come to California with me. That's all there is to it," Victor said. "And without your mother."

Dallas shook her head sadly. "We'll see."

When they went back to join the others, her mother had gone upstairs. Dallas only half-heartedly listened as the group discussed their plans. She knew that when everyone had left, she would have to deal with her mother.

She was almost relieved when the meeting broke up early. Before he left, Victor said, "Remember, you're coming with me. Just stick to that."

"We'll see," she said again, realizing that not even Victor could fully understand how she could hate her mother and sympathize with her at the same time. Once again her mother would play on her sympathy, making her feel guilty and sorry.

When she went upstairs, Dallas was not surprised to find her mother's light on and to hear a call from her room. Her mother was in bed with a book in her hand. "Come and sit down," Mrs. Davis said, patting the side of the bed and putting her book aside. "I think we have to have a talk."

"What's there to talk about?" Dallas sat on the edge of the bed.

"Don't start off that way. Why are you so hostile to me? Okay, that's a dumb question. I suppose all daughters sometimes feel that way about their mothers. I just wish you weren't going through that phase now, so soon after we lost Dad."

"Maybe you're the one going through a phase, not me," Dallas said.

Mrs. Davis sighed deeply. "If only it were a phase. I see my whole life stretching ahead, empty years —"

"Is that all you want to talk about?" Dallas asked, standing up.

"No. I want to talk about this trip to California. Is there any reason why we can't both go?"

"Yes. Lots of reasons. If you don't know them, I'm not going to spell them out. Let's forget it. I'm not going."

"You're being very unfair. You're not trying to understand my side of it."

"I do understand it. You don't want to be alone. You want to be with me every minute, and it's terrible." Dallas wanted to rush out of the room, but her mother reached over and took her hand.

"Don't be so harsh with me. Think about it, Dallas, think about my side of it. Think what a good time we could have on such a trip. Don't deprive us both."

"I'm not going," Dallas said. "Good night."

Alone in her room, Dallas sank down on her bed and tried to clear her thoughts. One thing she was sure of: she would not change her mind. She would not go on the trip if her mother insisted on coming along.

The next day was a work day for Dallas, and Jen came to the library to pick her up at five o'clock. As soon as they were alone outdoors, Jen said, "What are you going to do? About the trip, I mean."

"Nothing. I'm not going. I told my mother last night I wasn't going. She thinks I'm being unfair."

"That's the dumbest thing I ever heard. You've got to do something, Dallas."

Dallas felt her newly found strength ebbing. "I'm trapped. I've told you that before."

"No one has to be trapped who doesn't want to be. You've got to get out."

The girls parted at Dallas's corner, but Dallas kept on thinking about what Jen had said. On the spur of the moment she decided to stop in to see Vi Waters. She felt that maybe talking to her mother's friend would help.

Vi was very glad to see her and sat her down with a cup of hot tea. "I think of you a lot, and of course Victor tells me about you," Mrs. Waters said. "How are you doing?"

"I'm doing okay. It's my mother. She doesn't when a call came from her grandmother in seem to get any better. If anything, she's in a worse state now than right after my father died."

"I know. I try to get her to go out, but she won't. The boys told me she wants to go to California with all of you in the summer."

"I'm not going," Dallas said.

"Dallas, you know the kids don't want your mother along. I can see their point. But you should go. Why don't you?"

Dallas shook her head. "I can't."

"We'll see. Your mother has a birthday coming up in a few weeks. Why don't we give a party for her? I'll give it here. We'll surprise her. I'll invite all her old friends. Maybe if she sees that we all do care for her, she won't feel so alone. It can't hurt anyway."

"That's a good idea!" Dallas felt some hope. Perhaps Vi was the one who could really help.

In the next few days Dallas spent a lot of time with Vi Waters planning the party, sending out invitations, and helping with preparing her mother's favorite dishes that would be kept in the Waters' freezer until her mother's birthday.

A few days before the party, Dallas was home and her mother was at the beauty parlor Florida. "I'm coming up," she told Dallas. "I won't take no this time. I'll surprise your mother for her birthday. Don't tell her. It will be a happy surprise."

Dallas didn't know what to say. She didn't think it would be a happy surprise for her mother, but she didn't say so. Suddenly the idea sounded good to her, and she said, "Fine, Grandma. I'll meet you at the airport. Give me your flight and arrival time."

Dallas wrote down the information and wondered what excuse she would give her mother to take the car for an afternoon. She'd figure out something.

12

Ellen stood at the window and watched
Dallas drive off in the car. She had been mys-
terious about where she was going, but Ellen
hadn't pushed her to tell. She was quite sure
something was going on about her birthday
the next day. Dallas had been spending a lot
of time at the Waters' house, and there had
been much low-voiced telephoning. Ellen
liked the idea that that nice bunch of kids was
planning something for her. Although her
own daughter got annoyed with her, the young
people accepted her, even at the coming age
of thirty-eight.

Thirty-eight. In two years she'd be forty.
She might live until her seventies or eighties.
The thought of all those years extending
ahead made her spirits sink with despair. One
day was as empty as the next, one empty
afternoon like another. Mechanically she

turned to the television set and flicked it on. She poured herself another cup of coffee and sat down to watch the troubles of a fictional family.

She had fallen asleep on the sofa when the car coming into the driveway woke her up. Miraculously the afternoon had passed; she had gotten through another day. Already it was dark outside. She stood up, straightened her crumpled skirt, and turned off the TV. Dallas disapproved of her watching television, but Dallas didn't know how slowly the time passed, how agonizing each new day was. Dallas disapproved of her altogether, which seemed so unfair. She should be pleased that she had a young mother — comparatively young anyway — who wanted to be her friend. But Dallas didn't want her friendship; she never confided in her. She never allowed the nice, cozy, heart-to-heart talks a mother should have with her daughter. All her daughter's friends treated her like one of their own crowd, but not Dallas.

"Mom, where are you?" Dallas had come in the back door and was calling from the kitchen. Someone was with her.

Ellen went to the kitchen and then stopped dead still. She couldn't believe her eyes. "Mother! Good heavens, where did you come from?" It took her a few minutes to get over the shock.

"From the airport. I wanted to surprise you for your birthday." Her mother was kissing her, and Ellen could smell her mother's sweet scent that she had never liked.

"You certainly did surprise me. My goodness, it's a shock."

"I hope a pleasant one," her mother said. "Let me look at you." Eva Hendrix stood off at arm's length to examine her daughter. "You're too thin and you're pale. You're not eating enough."

"I eat plenty," Ellen said. She was examining her mother too. Mrs. Hendrix was a tall woman who still retained some of the prettiness her daughter and granddaughter had inherited. She had a full figure, which she had not let run to fat, and the same fine skin as the two younger women. Her imposing appearance made Ellen feel the same old mixture of pride in her mother's strength and the sense of inadequacy that it generated in her. If she lived to be a hundred, she thought, she would still feel overshadowed by her mother.

"This house is drafty," Mrs. Hendrix commented, taking off her coat. "I'm not used to this cold weather. Can you turn up the heat?"

"Oil is expensive," Ellen said.

"You're not so poor that we have to freeze. Dallas, turn up the thermostat. I'll take my things up to your room, Ellen. I can sleep in the other twin bed."

That she would not have, Ellen decided. "I don't think you'll be comfortable there, Mother. I get up a lot at night, and I sit up and read."

"I don't mind. I sleep very well. You won't disturb me."

"All right. You take my room, and I'll fix up a bed for myself on the sofa."

"I wouldn't hear of it. You just stay in your own bed, and you won't even know I'm there."

Small chance of that, Ellen thought.

Dallas spoke up. "Grandma, you take my room. I don't mind the sofa, I really don't. I like it."

"If you insist. I suppose you're young enough to sleep anyplace."

Ellen gave Dallas a quick squeeze of her hand and a murmured "Thank you," as she followed her mother up the stairs to her daughter's room.

It was a trying evening for Ellen. Her mind was flooded with memories of the times that her mother had come to visit when Hank was alive. He had been a protective shield for her. He had always been very kind to her mother, and her mother had adored him. Ellen had been grateful to him for being so considerate of his mother-in-law, catering to her in a way that Ellen never could. At the same time, however, she resented the way her mother had imposed on his good nature and at times wanted to shout at her, "He's doing it for me, not for you, you vain old woman."

Hank had laughed when she had admonished him not to let her mother take advantage of him. "I don't mind. She's not my mother — I don't have your old hang-ups — and she doesn't come that often."

Now, as the evening progressed, Ellen was amazed at how patient Dallas was with her grandmother. She was behaving very much like her father. Ellen was touched and a little amused, although her amusement was tinged with a streak of envy: Why was Dallas so gentle with her grandmother and so abrupt with her?

Ellen noticed the difference in Dallas's attiture right at the start when she and Dallas were preparing dinner. "Don't you have a cutting board?" her mother had demanded, watching Dallas cut vegetables on the counter.

"Yes, of course," Dallas said agreeably. "I forgot."

When she had brought out the board, Mrs. Hendrix then proceeded to show her how to use a knife to chop the vegetables finely.

"Dallas knows how to do it," Ellen said. "You'll make her so nervous she'll cut herself."

"I'm showing her how to do it right," her mother said.

"You make me nervous," Ellen mumbled.

"It's okay, Mom," said Dallas. "Why don't

you and Grandma sit down and have a glass of wine. I'll fix dinner." She gave them a smile.

"That's a good idea." Mrs. Hendrix put two glasses on a tray. "Let's go into the living room."

Ellen followed her mother, carrying the wine.

"You're a lucky woman to have such a daughter," her mother said with a sigh. "She's a wonderful girl."

"I know it," Ellen agreed, thinking immediately that her mother was implying she had a terrible daughter in Ellen. "She was very dear to stay home with me this year."

"You don't know what it means to be alone. Sometimes the loneliness gets so bad that you don't think you can live through another day."

Ellen ran her hand through her hair. She seemed to hear herself speaking. "I'm lonely even with Dallas here."

"But wait till she goes. Then you'll know what it's really like." Ellen almost laughed at the way her mother spoke: as if she *wanted* Ellen to know. "I was thinking, Ellen," her mother continued, "if I sold my condominium in Florida, I could add on a room and bath here for myself, and maybe we wouldn't have to be so lonely. Someday I may be too old to live alone."

"But you like Florida," Ellen said firmly, "and you don't like the cold weather."

"I could still go down for a couple of months in the winter. Maybe you'd come with me." Her tall, imposing mother, sitting erect in her chair, looked at her wistfully, but Ellen shrank from being taken in by her mother's wiliness. No, she said determinedly to herself, I am not going to end up living with my mother. She is a remarkable woman, and there's a lot to admire, but not for me to live with.

"I don't think it would be a good idea for us to live together," Ellen said.

"Why not? Why shouldn't a mother and daughter live together? Your daughter is living with you." Mrs. Hendrix's questions sounded like statements.

"Dallas is still very young," Ellen said defensively.

Not until Dallas had called them into the kitchen to eat, and they were sitting at the table, did the thought forcibly strike Ellen: Dallas hates living with me! Ellen had been pushing the realization from her mind ever since Dallas's anguished, blunt words when she had spoken about getting a job. She had tried to put Dallas's outcry down to a bad mood, because to accept what she had said as true was to be destroyed. Ellen felt she was very different from her mother: she wasn't forever criticizing Dallas or trying to change her. All she wanted was love and friendship. Maybe that's what every mother wanted from her daughter, and there was no right way to seek it. Surely Dallas loved her, or did one just take for granted that a daughter loved her mother? Did she love her mother? She hadn't thought about loving anyone except her husband and Dallas for a long time. Ellen felt that she had to stop and give the matter a lot of thought. Growing up, she had assumed that she loved her mother, and then, when she was adolescent and found her mother bossy and constantly critical, there had been a lot of arguments. But she wondered if she had stopped loving her. After she had married, her parents had moved to Florida, and her father had died, she hadn't thought much about her mother except for phone calls and visits — visits that Ellen had never looked forward to.

Sitting at the table between her daughter and her mother, Ellen thought, Here we are, three generations. Dallas doesn't get along with me well, and I don't get along with my mother well, and yet Dallas and her grandmother get along fine. She felt depressed by her thoughts and yet her mind kept worrying at them. She had read enough to know that the love between a mother and a daughter had a lot of ambiguities as she had said to Dallas when they were talking about the summer trip. Yet some daughters adored their mothers almost unconditionally. Perhaps she had never learned about love from her mother, had never learned that a parent's love had to be more giving than taking, and that one cannot take a child's love for granted. Maybe she had never really loved anyone but Hank. . . .

"You're very quiet, Ellen," her mother said.

"What's wrong with that?" was her sharp and automatic response. Oh, Lord, she thought, my mother is over sixty years old, and I am a married woman with a grown daughter. Will I ever get over reacting so strongly to her? "I was just thinking," she added more gently. "I'm sorry. What were you saying about your friends in Florida?"

Ellen listened patiently to a long tale her mother told about a luncheon she had been to, including a detailed explanation of what every woman had worn (people Ellen didn't know and never would know) , what they had eaten, and what her mother thought of each dish. Ellen had to keep reminding herself, She has no one to talk to at home. Naturally she wants to talk to us. I must be kind to her.

By the time Ellen was ready to go to bed she was exhausted. Her evening had been torn between irritation with her mother's insistent chatter and preoccupation with her own feelings, as well as an honest desire to try to make her mother's stay as pleasant as possible. Once she was in bed, however, she tried to figure out how she could diplomatically send her mother back to Florida in a few days. By the looks of her luggage she had come for at least several weeks.

They were both very sweet to her on her birthday. Dallas brought her breakfast in bed, and her mother insisted on taking her out to lunch. She was with the two people in the world closest to her, and yet her longing for Hank colored her whole day gray. The awful thing was, she thought, that the times she had enjoyed most before, family holidays and festivities, now were the most painful.

Dallas said that she couldn't lunch with them; she had some other things to do. "I'll pick up something for dinner tonight," Ellen said.

"No, I'll take care of it. You're not supposed to do anything today."

Dallas wasn't very good at lying, and Ellen was positive that something was in the air for the evening. She wasn't surprised when later in the day Dallas said they'd go out to eat and that, since it was a celebration, they should all get dressed up.

Before getting dressed, Ellen stretched out on her bed to rest. At lunch her mother had spoken again of selling her apartment and coming up North to live with Ellen. Ellen had felt her defenses breaking down. After all, what difference would the change make? She didn't think she could be unhappier than she already was, so how she lived or with whom didn't matter. She was ready to give up. Hank was gone, and what happened to her was unimportant.

Ellen had never felt so depressed in her life, and in a way the attempts by her mother and Dallas to celebrate her birthday made things even worse. But she got up and took a shower and got dressed. Perhaps a party with those young friends of Dallas would cheer her up. At least, they made her feel that she wasn't ready to be put on the shelf quite yet.

"You look lovely, Mom," Dallas said to her, when she came downstairs.

But her mother had to spoil the compliment. "I don't think you ought to wear earrings and a gold chain. I'd take off the earrings if I were you."

"I like them," Ellen said. "I'm not you."

Her mother looked disapproving.

"We're going to stop at the Waters' for a few minutes. Vi called when you were out and invited us for a drink before we go to dinner," Dallas said in the car.

"That's nice," said Ellen.

Ellen knew before they went into the house that there was going to be a party. All the lights were on, and she could see the people.

But when she stepped into the entrance hall, and everyone came out shouting "Surprise" and "Happy Birthday," she truly was surprised. She had simply assumed that the party was going to be given by Dallas and her young friends, but instead here were all the couples that she had been avoiding since Hank died. She was completely taken aback, but she tried to cover her dismay as well as possible. She hugged Vi, let everyone kiss her, and introduced her mother around.

In the living room there was a bar set up and there were beautiful canapes. Ellen hoped that she could shake her depression now compounded by her disappointment. But she wasn't doing a good job of it. She still felt alienated from her old friends; the women all had their husbands and she had her mother. Undoubtedly they were all feeling sorry for her, and too many of them said, "It's nice for you to have your mother visiting," as if to have her mother was some great treat for poor, little, lonely Ellen. Yucky, thought Ellen, borrowing one of the kids' words.

And, as Ellen was being reminded, her mother was the kind of woman who made her presence felt. Unabashedly she asked personal questions and made opinionated comments. Everyone was polite to her, but Ellen could see her mother fasten onto one person after another. No sooner did one make an excuse to get away than her mother, undaunted, would find another ear for her compulsive talking and carry on. I am not responsible for her, Ellen told herself, but yet she felt that she was. Between worrying about her mother boring everyone and her own discomfort, she wished that the evening would end. But there was still a buffet supper ahead.

While supper was being served, Andy and Victor joined them. Ellen watched them fill their plates and promptly get hold of Dallas, who had been helping with the serving. They maneuvered her to a small table, where the three of them sat down. Ellen was just about to get a plate for herself and join them when her mother beat her to them. She could hear her mother's loud, clear voice. "My, how you two boys — or I should say young men — have grown. Now you must tell me all about yourselves. I'm going to sit here with you. I don't have much opportunity to dine with two such handsome young men."

Andy and Vic looked embarrassed but made a place for her, and the four of them sat at the small, crowded table.

Ellen tried to shrug off her mother's appropriation of the three young people. Let her have a good time, she thought. But as the meal came to an end, and her mother continued to monopolize the two men — Dallas left the table and was helping Vi clear the plates away

— she grew annoyed and began to feel that she should do something to rescue them. But, she argued with herself, it was not her problem; it was theirs. However, her eyes kept going back to them.

"Your mother seems to be enjoying herself with the boys," Vi said to her.

"She's probably boring them stiff," said Ellen.

"It won't hurt them. They're good-natured with older people. I hate to see kids be rude, although I don't believe in asking too much of them. I don't like to see older people make fools of themselves — " Her friend stopped suddenly, and Ellen could see she had said more than she'd intended.

"Like who?" Ellen demanded. "Are you trying to tell me something?"

"Tonight's your birthday. Let's talk about it some other time." Vi was looking at her, and Ellen knew that Vi would not lie to her.

"What's there to talk about? You think I've been making a fool of myself with the kids?" Ellen followed Vi into the kitchen, where they were alone.

"I think you've been hurting yourself. The people here tonight are your friends; they care about you. You've been running away, and I think you should stop."

"I suppose the boys told you that I want to

go on the trip to the coast with them this summer."

"Yes, they did." Vi, who had been busy at the sink, swung around to face her. "Don't push it, Ellen. You'll get hurt."

"You mean they don't want me?"

Vi nodded her head. "None of them will go if you go along. The trip will be called off."

Ellen stood still. Feeling shaky, she balanced herself against the kitchen counter. She was glad that Vi kept busy with the dishes and did not try to comfort her. The blow had been coming for a long time, like a tornado that one sees whirling in the distance, and now it had landed with all its force and hit her.

Of course it was true. She had known it was true, but she had kept on kidding herself. She was as bad as her mother, worse. Her mother was trying to hold on to her, and she had desperately been clinging to Dallas. And her clinging had been worse because she had used not only her daughter but her daughter's friends. How Dallas must hate her. The last thought choked her throat.

"Don't think about it now," Vi said. "Let's go back and join the others."

"I'll be along in a few minutes," Ellen said.

She went to the bathroom and washed her face and reapplied her makeup. Before she went out, she sat for a few moments on the edge of the tub and thought about her husband. She felt that he was close to her. She could almost hear him saying, "You've had a rough time, darling, but you're going to be on the right track now." She prayed to God that she would be.

Ellen had had only one cocktail before dinner, and now she took a liqueur and sat down to talk with the guests. Victor and Dallas had disappeared. She didn't know where and she was not going to ask, and her mother was still bending Andy's ear. She had thought the liqueur would relax her, but the tensions of the evening were more than a small glass of cherry brandy could cure. She was trying to fight down a tremendous anger against her mother. Her mother's bossiness, her constant criticism had taught her nothing above love, nothing about how a relationship between a mother and a daughter should be.

But could anyone teach that to another human being?

"Are you all right?" Bob Waters came and sat beside her. "You look worried."

"Not worried. Just thinking. I'm not used to it," she added with a little laugh. "We take so many things for granted, don't we?"

"You mean like life just going on? Are you thinking about Hank?"

"No, strangely enough, I'm not. I was thinking about Dallas. About mothers and daughters. I haven't been very good to Dallas since Hank died."

"She's very devoted to you."

"Maybe. But that's what we take for granted: that our children love us. They don't have to, do they?" She was studying Bob's face.

"Most children love their parents. But parents have to be wise in knowing what to accept. A parent has to help a kid break loose when the time comes."

Ellen knew he was choosing his words carefully, and she did not say anything. What was the use of trying to defend herself?

When the party started to break up, Ellen looked around for Dallas, but neither she nor Victor were in sight. She went to gather her mother to go home.

"Where's Dallas?" Mrs. Hendrix asked.

"I don't know. I guess she's gone off somewhere with Victor."

"What do you mean you don't know? She's your daughter. You should know where she is."

"Mother, come on. It's time for us to go home."

"You're not going to leave without Dallas!"

"She knows how to get home. Please, Mother, everyone is leaving. I'm tired, and I'm sure the Waters are." Ellen turned to say goodbye to her friends and to kiss both Vi and Bob warmly. "It was a beautiful party. And," she whispered to Vi, "an extraordinary evening for me. I'll never forget it."

"Would you like me to drive you home

since Dallas isn't here?" Andy offered. "I don't mind walking back."

"No, thank you, Andy. I can drive. No problem."

Andy had warned her too. In his half-insolent, teasing way, he had been telling her she was on the wrong track. She felt mortified that she had been attracted to him, had flirted with him. Andy was the last person she wanted to be with that night.

Ellen practically had to pull her mother away, still insisting indignantly that she could not understand her daughter going home without Dallas.

13

"It's nice to be here alone with you," Dallas said, looking across the table at Victor. They had slipped out of the Waters' house to get some air, and then, on the spur of the moment, decided to go for a ride and ended up at a coffeehouse.

"It's nice to be with you." Victor grinned. "I'm hungry."

"After all that food at your mother's!"

"That was a long time ago." He ordered a cheeseburger for himself and sodas for them both. Dallas insisted she was still full.

Dallas felt herself unwinding. "I don't think my mother enjoyed her party very much," she said.

"Your mother doesn't enjoy anything very much, does she? Has she said anything more about the trip? You've got to go."

"I don't see how I can." Dallas shook her head. "She'd figure out a way to come along."

"No way. You've got to level with her. Tell her that no one wants a mother to come. Not any mother. This problem has got to be settled once and for all. I'm marrying you, not you and your mother. Don't you see, honey, if you don't tell her now, it's only going to get worse."

"You think it's easy. . . ."

"I don't. Believe me. I think you're fantastic to have put up with what you have. All right, I know why you have, but at some point you'll become plain self-destructive, and that point is now. You've got to take a stand."

"Jen says that too. . . . I kept hoping the situation would work itself out, that she would see what she was doing. But I guess nothing is going to happen by itself." Dallas had been leaning against the back of the booth, but now she sat up straight. "I'm going to do it. I'm going to make the break."

Victor picked up her hand. "Now you're talking. Promise?"

"I'm not promising you. I'm promising myself." She felt a surge of confidence. "I'm really going to do it. I'll tell her."

They talked about other things, but Dallas's mind kept going back to her mother. She was thinking aloud when she said, "I didn't mind staying home this year. I think my mother really did need me. But I didn't figure on her taking me over so totally, me and my friends — " She looked up at Victor and laughed. "I guess I'm rehearsing what to say."

"You're doing okay. What are you so nervous about?"

"I want to say what I have to say, but I don't want to hurt her. It's funny, when I'm away from her, I feel that I love her. Then when I'm with her, I feel I can't stand her. Do your feelings ever change that way?"

"I don't think about the family the way you do. I guess having your father die made you think about a lot of things you didn't before."

"It sure did. Like feeling responsible for my mother. I never felt that before. I suppose that's part of loving, but it can be a terrible burden."

"Loving you is easy," Victor said with a grin.

When Dallas looked at her watch, she was startled to find it was almost midnight. "We'd better go. My mother will be having a fit wondering where I am."

They drove past Victor's house and saw that all the cars were gone and that the house was almost dark. "My mother will be furious that we didn't get back before everyone left," Dallas said nervously. "She'll tell me I spoiled her birthday party."

"Don't worry about what she tells you. It's what you have to tell her that's important,"

Victor said, and stretched his hand out to squeeze hers.

Dallas was not surprised that all the lights were on in her house and, after she kissed Victor good-night and went inside, that both her mother and grandmother were waiting up for her.

"I'm sorry, Mom. I didn't realize it was so late." Dallas looked apologetically from one to the other.

"I should think you would be sorry," her grandmother said tartly. "Where in the world were you? Disappearing like that, and staying out until midnight."

"Vi knew I went out with Victor. We just started to go for a little air, and then he got hungry and we stopped and got to talking." Dallas gave her explanation breathlessly.

"Did you have a nice time?" her mother asked quietly. "I'm glad you have Victor. He's a good person."

"I don't think it was very good of him to take her off like that," Mrs. Hendrix said crossly. "From your party, Ellen."

"It was my party, not hers. You and Vi did a beautiful job, Dallas, and it was a lovely surprise. I really thank you." Her mother seemed preoccupied, and Dallas wondered what she was thinking. Mrs. Davis turned to her mother. "Why don't you go up to bed, Mother? I want to talk to Dallas for a bit."

Now the reaction would come, Dallas

thought. Her mother would do her scolding in private.

"Hmmph," was all her grandmother replied, but she said good-night and went up the stairs to her bedroom.

Dallas sat down and watched her mother take off her earrings and shake out her hair. She didn't want to get into an argument, and she decided she had better speak her mind first, before her mother started to scold her for leaving the party. "I want to talk to you," Dallas said firmly. "I've made up my mind to go to California with the kids, but not if you come. I'm not going to baby-sit for you anymore. You've used me, you've used my friends, you've taken over my life until it's unbearable. I've got to lead my own life, and I hope you can lead yours. I can't replace Dad, and I don't want to try. Maybe you're going to hate me, to think I'm a terrible daughter, but I can't help it. I've stuck it out as long as I can, and now I've got to take a stand. You talk about being friends — I hope we *can* be friends — but you want to own me, and that's not love or friendship."

She stopped, breathless, her heart hammering. Dallas was afraid to look at her mother. When she did, her mother was curled up on the sofa, her shoes kicked off and her feet tucked under her. She looked young and vulnerable, the way she had the day in the hospital when Dallas's father had died.

Her mother spoke slowly. "I suppose I have this coming to me. What can I say? I'm not surprised. You've been trying to tell me this right along, but I didn't want to hear it. I haven't faced anything, Dallas. I haven't faced that Hank is dead, I haven't faced being alone. I've been putting everything off. I couldn't even buy a new bedspread. I'm glad you had the courage to come out with what you think. I probably never could."

"I'm sorry it has to be this way," Dallas said.

"Don't be sorry," her mother said fiercely. "Be glad that you're young and have a strong sense of life. I've been feeding on your strength and that's wrong. I have to find my own."

"Why don't you have Grandma come up to live with you?" Dallas asked.

Her mother shook her head. "No, I need to be alone. Maybe someday when my mother is too old to live by herself, I'll be able to take her on, but first I have to find my own way." Her mother looked at her thoughtfully. "It's funny, isn't it? I seem more the adolescent than you. I guess growing up has little to do with age." She cupped her chin in her hand. "Sometimes you know you're doing something wrong, but you keep on doing it, unable to stop. Many times I could actually hear myself saying things I knew I shouldn't have. I hope I can stop, Dallas, but people don't change overnight. All I can do is try."

"That's doing a lot. And you won't really be alone. I mean you're not getting rid of me altogether. Even if I go away to school in the fall, or when I get married, we'll always be mother and daughter."

Her mother laughed. "I guess you're stuck with that. Your father would be proud of you, Dallas. You're solid and strong. But that's enough for now, I'll make up the sofa for your bed."

"I'll help you." But first Dallas stopped and looked at her mother searchingly. "You're going to be okay, Mom, you will. And thank you, thank you, very much. I hope you had a good birthday."

"It turned out better than I thought it would," Ellen said.

But there was a sad, lonely look on her mother's face that Dallas knew would be a long time in fading. Yet Dallas was certain that she could not be the one to erase it. She could only hope that eventually the pain would diminish and that her mother would find her own way.

About the Author

Hila Colman grew up in New York City and was graduated from Radcliffe College. After college, she did publicity and promotion work; then she wrote articles for magazines and eventually she began to write books. She has been writing books for teenagers for many years. "I love teenagers," she says, "I am on their side because they are fluid, fermenting, and rich with life and living."

She lives in Bridgewater, Connecticut where she is extremely active in the town's government. Her new book, GIRL MEETS BOY will soon be available from Scholastic, Inc. in a Vagabond edition.